Out of the Fog

J. Carl Go

<u>WHAT READERS HAVE SAID...</u>

Carl's book is just what I've been looking for! As a Senior who is a fan of mysteries it is a great read!

Don Sundquist
Governor of Tennessee
1995 – 2003

A fictional story that is very entertaining and interesting but pulls at your heartstrings. This really happens in today's real world as many senior citizens are being abused and their possessions and wealth is being stolen. A highly recommended read that will stimulate your thinking and remind you of events happening every day with our loved ones!

R.A. Tiebout
Lt. General, USMC (Retired)

Lost sleep; out of touch; months; survival; yes, turn the page and hurry! Lots of questions; few answers. Lock the door; don't trust anyone; him, her, who? Caring, trusting, brave, more lost sleep. Can't put it down; read on! True friends, joy, happiness, challenges, intense! Changes; waiting; impressive; good and bad; patience; looking up; good thinking! Impressive decisions; three heads better than one; lock your doors! Good advice; best friends; super settlement! Rewards deserved; trio's friendship for life; nothing better! Bookshelves soon; Best Seller #1! More, more!

June A.

Retired

Out of the Fog

J. Carl Goodman

CONTENTS

FORWORD

This is my first ever book... I hope it doesn't show too much. A dream inspired this; yes, a dream. Like many of you, I do dream but don't remember much upon awakening. In this case, the dream that occurred two years ago as of this writing was so vivid that I remembered it in detail. I shared it with my dear friend Walt, and rather than razz me about it; he thought it was a good story. I decided shortly afterwards that I would write this book. I was so involved in my long-standing Human Resources firm that time was at a premium. Due to the Covid, and a subsequent business slowdown, I found the time to write.

One of the reasons I chose to write this is that I have had an awareness of the issues surrounding ageing in America and how it affects all of us. Being a senior at 72, I also consider myself to be at least at present, a formidable and contributing force for my company, for my clients, my family, for my friends and my community and church. I felt it necessary to portray The Team as such.

In addition, the problems that beset seniors are myriad. Here is some data to pique your interest. In 2019, 16.5% of our population were over age 65; 34% were over 50. Over the last decade, the number of those over 65 grew by 35% (2020 U.S. Census)! Seniors are the fastest-growing demographic. In fact, 10,000 Americans turn 65 every day; that's right, every day! Being a senior certainly doesn't render one feeble or mentally unreliable. In fact, I'm sure that very few people consider Tom Selleck, Sly Stallone, Tommy Lee Jones, Mark Harmon, Liam Neeson or Bruce Willis over the hill. Oh, and how about Joan Collins, Morgan Freeman, Samuel Jackson, Clint Eastwood, Blythe Danner and Helen Mirren?!

Now for some more factual data that is not as pleasant. One in six people over 60 within a safe and familiar community are abused! The types of abuse include financial, physical, emotional, neglect and sexual. Of those abuses, only 1 of 14 cases are reported to law enforcement; and only 1 in 44 cases of financial abuse are reported! The fraud and theft costs exceed $3BB each year! 60% of abusers are family members. Financial abuse is rampant. Examples include stealing cash, jewelry, identity, and credit cards. Victims are often misled into giving money. Forgery and abuse of powers of attorney, wills and legal documents are common. Overdoses of medication, being hit with objects, yelling and threatening comments, and even sexual abuse occur.

What surprises me is that even in upscale and expensive independent living or assisted living situations where the resident is paying much for their care, they cannot always trust the nurses, aides, caregivers, cleaners and maintenance people with their money, jewelry and valuables. Would it not be awful to have lived a good life and to have acquired nice things that one cannot have with them? To have a situation where one cannot leave their purse or wallet with cash in their room or apartment because those entrusted with keys may steal from them? To make one's home in a place where your nice watch or jewelry has a strong likelihood of being stolen? To feel like your own residence is not secure.

I don't know about you, but I hope you will find this book fun and entertaining while helping to build awareness of some of the issues facing seniors. Let's make seniors a priority!

I also wanted to use The Team to demonstrate that we all need friendships and relationships that are endearing and lasting, even through difficult times. Each of us needs others.

I felt that even in a story of mystery and adventure, there are lessons and demonstrations of right and wrong; good and evil; and the consequences of such. I hope you have fun with this book and feel good at the end.

But with all this, remember that "Out of the Fog" is entirely fictional!

I hope you enjoy this story. I'm already working on The Team's next adventure with, *The Dysfunctional Family*.

How It Began

Harvey England smiled to himself as he drove his pickup toward home, an upscale condo he had purchased three years ago. It had been a good day. After retiring four years ago at the age of seventy and selling his successful civil engineering firm, he found he enjoyed speaking with engineering students about their choices and options for their careers. Today had been a good group of students with much enthusiasm and right questions. While he did such talks three or four times a year, this was one of the better groups. Harv's firm had been highly successful working commercial and government projects, so he was knowledgeable regarding a variety of engineering practices: surveying, layout and design, drainage, vertical building codes, environmental and remediation practices, etc. Also, because of his firm working with many large manufacturing companies, he was in tune with the issues of manufacturing, lean practices, OSHA, and the regulations that surrounded his practice. It meant that the community college, Parkland, felt he was an asset that was perfect to exploit... and the students loved it.

During the drive, however, Harv felt that physically something wasn't right; he felt a bit odd and different. He could not quite place the feeling. It wasn't a cold coming on; it wasn't indigestion or nausea. He became anxious to get home. It was mid-January and cold outside, but there was no snow on the ground.

Harv lived alone since his beloved wife, Margaret, had died from cancer five years prior. Even though he had eventually learned how to live without her, he couldn't live in the house they shared for so many years, so he purchased the condo. It was very nice with about 2,500 square feet with two master bedroom suites and a nice, open, and large living area. With a 2½ car garage, it was perfect for working on his vehicles. The home was decorated with much of the furniture and mementos of their lives, travels, and family together. Margaret's passion was fine stained glass so her several original Tiffany lamps were on display beautifully. Harv deeply appreciated Margaret's eye for quality and the beauty of the lamps, but his interest in woodworking, sports, and time spent on and in his beautiful red 1965 Mustang convertible sometimes seemed at odds with Margaret's more gentile tastes. So it was.

Harv pulled his pickup into the garage, closed the main garage door, and entered the house through a side door into a hallway connecting to the kitchen. He hung up his coat on a peg attached to a hallway mirror and walked into the living room. He realized that he was still feeling poorly, and his thinking was disjointed and not cohesive. He thought, *'Maybe I should call someone.'* Harvey had a severe headache that came on from nowhere. His neck was so stiff within a short time that it hurt to even look down or to the side; and he was shivering severely. He wondered what could possibly be wrong.

That was the last he remembered!

What about Harvey?

Harvey England was born in central Illinois, Champaign to be exact. His father was a hard-working auto mechanic who did well and became the Service Manager for one of the largest GM dealerships in the Midwest. Harvey's only sibling, a younger sister, Emma, was killed in an awful auto accident when she was ten and he was fourteen. It was very traumatic for him; in fact, throughout his life, he was fraught with pangs of emotion and realized that he missed her more than he had ever suspected.

Harv focused his attention on education and went on to the University of Illinois graduating in Civil Engineering with an outstanding GPA. He was always extremely competitive with an intense desire to stand out and win, but those characteristics were combined with his mom's concern for others and fair treatment which made Harv a well-rounded person. The university atmosphere along with intramural athletics and service organizations helped him develop his whole person and personality. Harv was a standout runner and, while he was tall and lanky as a student, he was a notable wrestler as well. He made friends easily and helped them by modeling a balance of priorities. He continued throughout his life to credit his mother for that.

Harv knew that although the family lived a middle-class life, college would be financially hard on them, even at an in-state school. The Army ROTC was appealing to Harvey so he accepted an ROTC scholarship that would pay his tuition along with a little spending money each month for his commitment to serve on active duty as an officer upon graduation. Both his folks were very hesitant because in 1964 when Harv graduated from Champaign Central High, the Vietnam War was claiming too many young soldiers and promised to take more. Harv's parents continued to worry, and as Harvey approached his third year in college and ROTC, he had an accident playing flag football with some friends and broke his left shoulder. He was told he could not continue with his ROTC scholarship until his doctor gave the OK to return to duty. His parents were thrilled and thought it was their release from worry about Harvey going off to Vietnam. Little did they know!

Harv worked two part-time jobs over the last two years of school to pay for his tuition, books, and fees but lived at home to save expenses. The good news was that due to his major in

Civil Engineering, one of his professors referred him to a friend who owned a surveying company. They hired Harv and paid him well over the going rate which enabled Harv to focus on his studies. He graduated in 1968 with his bachelor's degree which made his family and friends proud.

Shortly after his graduation, with some visits to family and friends, lots of internal turmoil, and thoughts about the next steps in his life, Harv came home one afternoon to announce that he had enlisted in the U.S. Army!

The family was in turmoil! Why did he enlist when his education and skills would have likely provided him with a good job and a good living? Why would he place his life at risk knowing that he was probably going to go to Vietnam? Why would he do that to his parents, family, and friends? Why would he enlist when he did not have to?

He tried to explain that his two years of ROTC training taught him so much about not just how to be a good college student, but about being a whole person. He spoke to them and others about how there was a sense of community, of helping others through difficulties, about examining his integrity and character. Harv was convinced that if four years of college helped him to mature, how much more he would grow and learn in the Army. But he also understood that they were worried about him. They were concerned for his safety. And to top it off, they were more perplexed when he told them he had enlisted for 4 years (instead of 2) to choose his specialty and training in combat engineering!

Harvey knew that even with the conflict in their feelings, his parents were proud of him and loved him. It was a very emotional time during the several weeks before he had to report for basic training.

After graduating from basic training, he went on to advanced training in what the army called both vertical (buildings, homes, etc.) and horizontal (roads, drainage, bridges, landing strips, etc.) construction and became a great asset to their team. Due to his education and his work experience in addition to the military training, he did very well. In the military, every person is a soldier first regardless of his/her occupation and Harv was adept in his use of weapons and close order combat in addition to engineering. As suspected, upon completion of his training, Harv was sent to Vietnam where he spent a year. He never spoke much of his experience there like so many other war veterans. Upon returning stateside, or back to *the world* as they said, he was assigned to Fort Carson in Colorado where he enjoyed performing on-base construction projects and during his last year was the non-commissioned officer in charge of many. Harv often reflected quietly on how far he had come in thought, knowledge, maturity, and discipline since he started college in '64. Everything was different now in 1972.

Everyone was joyful at Harv's homecoming! They were hoping that he would find a good job within an easy commute of Champaign. Harvey utilized the help of the university's Career Services office and learned of several opportunities. For his interests, the best fit seemed to be with a company called Brown & Root, headquartered in Baton Rouge, LA with the job based in Houston, Texas. He interviewed and they offered him a position with an outstanding salary for that era and off he went. The company gave him great experience and skills in design, project management, working with construction vendors, environmental and air quality issues, budgets, etc.

After his move to Houston, he returned about six months later to attend the wedding of a good college friend. Wouldn't you know, that during the reception he reconnected with a friend from Champaign Central High, Margaret King. They danced, laughed, and recalled both the good times and personal challenges that beset them during those years. They hit it off extraordinarily well. In fact, Harv was not ready to go back to Houston and work after the weekend. But phone calls and visits became regular things for the two of them; and over the next year and a half, they had fallen deeply in love.

Harvey's parents loved her also. She was a motivated and multi-talented woman who had a very realistic view of life. As a professional Artist, she had gone back to Champaign after graduating from Eastern Illinois University and taught Art at their own Champaign Central High School; and she loved her work.

Then Harv asked her to marry him and the usual turmoil began. Would she have to move to Houston? Could she find a job that she could enjoy? Was she ready for such a move? How would her parents feel even though they loved Harv? The answers came easily because of both Harv's and Margaret's practical and pragmatic approach. They would marry; they would move to Houston, and they would thrive.

The Houston move in late '73 wasn't as difficult as they had expected. Harvey was making an excellent salary and through his friends at Brown & Root Margaret was soon teaching Art at one of the better high schools in the area. They bought a nice house and settled in. The England family of Houston was good and doing well.

Harv excelled at Brown & Root and was promoted throughout the various divisions. He managed people and projects for the "oil patch" and worked with the most common of "household name" energy companies. He did travel often and sometimes too far away for too long. It was hard when he would call home to find some new milestone had been achieved while he was away from home. He however remained a loyal employee. The company treated him well. Things changed in 1985. Harvey got a new boss. While Harv got along with everyone well and had a stellar reputation, his new boss did not like the kudos and notes that he would receive as the Director of Engineering Services commending his Manager of Capital Projects, Harvey England. He wanted the kudos for himself. It became hard for Harv and his boss to be cordial to one another and that reflected in Harv's most recent performance appraisal comments.

Also, in the mix was that Margaret's dad, Blake King, was struggling after experiencing a stroke. Harv and Margaret were regularly traveling back to Champaign to visit and assist her parents. It was so much nicer than the traffic and intensity of living in Houston. Between Harvey's conflicts with his current boss and both of their concerns about the King family, they discussed moving back to Illinois. Harvey was convinced that with his experience working with the largest and most successful clients in the business and with the sophisticated knowledge he had gained over 4 years in the military and 13 years with Brown & Root, he could be successful starting his own company.

Margaret and Harvey agreed. The move was on.

The England's were able to find a nice house that more than met their needs in a neighborhood in the Kirby and Mattis area. Margaret had been on the phone before their move speaking with her friends at Champaign Central High School. She learned that there was a new job opening at Champaign Centennial High School and after the awful administrative processes for application, she had the job.

Harvey was a bit gob smacked at how to start his firm, so he resorted to his strength, analysis. After deciding what to name it, what it would do for clients, how it would charge, and raise revenue, he focused on developing a detailed business plan. He didn't need to borrow money because they had been very diligent in saving. But he also knew that he would have to quickly get to work generating revenue. He also had learned that clients who were larger, commonly known companies of fine reputation would associate him with quality and, upon the completion of a project, there would more likely be additional work to be done. With that he found an excellent building to lease for his offices that had additional space into which he could grow as England Projects, LLC required more room. Harv felt great ...he was off to the races!

England Projects, LLC was still in 2020 a considerably successful engineering firm with an excellent reputation since its inception in 1985. He was proud of the firm's accomplishments and assistance to their clients. He had a wonderful team of managers and employees who were like friends and family. Margaret had become ill with breast cancer in 2002 and finally succumbed to the dreaded disease in 2015. As she entered her most difficult times with the disease in 2014, Harv spent less and less time at work and more time with her. His employees were more than able to run the firm in his absence. After she died, Harv found he no longer had the necessary interest in his company, probably he surmised, due to his age, years spent working, and the loss of his Margaret. Fortunately for Harvey, when he confided this to his two top managers, they returned the following week with a lucrative offer to buy the firm, including a nice percentage of the profits for the next 15 years. Along with his considerable savings and investments, Harvey was left financially advantaged.

He occupied his time with woodworking, his Mustang, working out at the gym, reading, and working with students at the college. Harvey was still a very formidable man even in his mid-70's.

Harvey's Back

His awareness was very fuzzy. Harvey had no idea where he was, whether it was day or night, what day it was or what time it was. His eyes were still closed but he realized that he was back from a long period of sleep or lack of consciousness. He was almost afraid to open his eyes; he did not even think about it. He listened hard; he was able to smell something neither pleasant nor unpleasant. He heard things. Something clanging in the distance, some footsteps maybe; there was a radio or TV on someplace. The only thing that registered is that he was not someplace familiar to him. He took a deep breath and faded again into sleep. Harvey's breathing tube had been removed several weeks prior when he demonstrated the ability to breathe on his own.

Harv awakened again. How long since his first awakening? Who knew? But he was again aware of sounds, smells, and the feeling of not knowing. This time he opened his eyes. He tried to lift his head to look around but did not have the strength ...his head felt so heavy. He was able to roll his head to the left side. He saw some windows on a wall close to his bed with blinds that were closed. He then rolled his head to the right. There was a door, 1/3rd ajar, that seemed to open onto a hallway, with a tile floor. There were obvious sounds of some movement not too far away. On his right index finger was something clamped to the end that had a wire leading to the wall behind him, but he could not see what was there. He was too fuzzy to realize that it was an oximeter that was plugged into an instrument with an alarm. But even at that point, Harvey knew it was something medical. Was he in the hospital? For what?

He was aware that in the hospital there are call buttons for the nurses. He looked around on either side of the bed but saw nothing. He suddenly realized that he was extremely thirsty. He thought he would just get out of bed and find something to drink. But then he realized he simply did not have the strength. What in the hell was wrong?

It was a horrible feeling to be seemingly alone in an unknown place, to be totally unknowing and physically helpless. Harv laid back on the bed and made the first noise that had come from his mouth since he awakened. A frustrated growl combined with a scream of helplessness left his body with significant volume and rage. People came running!

Were these nurses, doctors, aides? Harvey didn't know and didn't care ...there were several of these people in his room, all wearing face masks. They had faces of amazement and utterances of awe. The woman closest to him asked, "Are you all right? Do you need anything?" Harvey took a moment to find his voice and to say the words. "I'm so thirsty," he said. "I need a drink". The nurse turned to another in the room and told her to get him some cool water. As that person left, the head nurse, Brenda according to her name tag, asked Harvey, "When did you wake up? How are you feeling? Can you tell me your name and where you are?"

He looked at her and said, "I'm Harv England and woke up some minutes ago. I have no idea where I am or why I'm here. Please tell me." His throat felt very raw and scratchy when he spoke.

Brenda gave him a sorrowful and pitiful look, patted his left arm, and said, "Mr. England, you contracted a terrible case of Meningitis. While you were in the hospital and even after, the Dr.'s didn't think you would ever survive. Do you remember any of that?" After Harvey shook his head slightly, she continued. "Once the hospital determined that you were no longer contagious and they thought they could no longer do anything for you, they sent you here to us. You are in Wildstone Senior Living Community in the nursing care unit. You've been here for over 3 months now.

Brenda was getting ready to tell him some more, but a man in a suit, looking quite stern, came into the room and said, "That's quite enough, Brenda. He is probably in no condition to hear or remember your story." About that time, the other man arrived with Harvey's water. As he drank, Harv moaned, "Thanks." The water tasted and felt good going down his throat. As he drank slowly on purpose, he was trying to get his mind around what he had just heard. He didn't remember getting sick, being in the hospital, coming to this place, or anything about the last three-plus months. He was reeling!

The man in the suit introduced himself. "Mr. England, my name is Anthony Culpepper and I'm the Chief Administrator for Wildstone Senior Living Community. I am the one who will decide on your care. These people all work for me." Even in Harv's early state of awareness and sense of being back among people, he felt Mr. Culpepper was arrogant and a power-monger. Harv said nothing in response. Mr. Culpepper went on, "so please tell me how you feel?" Harvey responded, "I'm weak and it feels like I'm starting all over again. I appreciate your responsibility, Mr. Culpepper, but I absolutely do not work for you and I am an independent person with a sharp mind, a strong will, and hopefully soon, a strong body. I'm tired now and would like to be alone. Oh, by the way, nice suit. Brenda, could you remain for a moment?"

Anthony Culpepper was clearly surprised and recognized the sarcasm in Harvey's voice. In fact, he was surprised that Harv could be that sharp having just become part of the present company. Harv already knew he was not going to like this man. Mr. Culpepper had even, before Harv's awakening, worried about this happening, meaning Harvey's awakening, and how he may have to deal with it. It created a real problem for him! He left the room in a huff.

Brenda remained and asked, "How can I help you? Are you hungry? Uncomfortable?" Harvey kept it simple. He liked Brenda already and felt OK about expressing his feelings. "Brenda, I do not like that man and don't want him near me." Brenda just nodded in affirmation. Harv then asked, "Because I feel like I've lost months in my memory, please put a TV in my room right away so I can catch up on the news and get me a newspaper subscription. And, what's this tube coming down my leg?" Brenda responded with a chuckle, "That's a catheter, Mr. England. You've been in bed without the ability to get up for over 3 months here." Harvey immediately responded, "Well, get it the hell out of me now!"

"I will very soon. But before we do that you must be able to go to the bathroom safely and independently. Do you think you can do it now?" Harvey turned red with frustration and huffed, "I can't even lift my damn head off the pillow. But I'll be practicing until I can." Brenda replied with great tact, "We will have a Physical Therapist start working with you tomorrow to get you moving again. I'm sure it won't be long. In the meantime, I'll have an orderly get you a TV and a newspaper. Lots of things have happened since you got here. You may find it a bit frustrating! Try not to look at the politics she said with a chuckle. I'll also have a little food prepared for you" she said as she left the room.

Thoughts were bouncing around Harvey's brain like rocks in a rock tumbler. He thought, "Meningitis? Me? How? From where? Over 3 months here? How long in the hospital? Where? Oh, I'd better ask about that. Why is that Culpepper guy so arrogant? Why is he even interested in me? Brenda seems OK. So what day is it? What month? What time? I have to ask all that."

As his thoughts rolled along, Harv also tried to roll over repeatedly and to move in his hospital type bed. He tried to roll from his back onto his left side; back to center and then to his right side. Man, it was hard work. He caught his breath and lifted his legs. That was even harder. He lifted his arms from his side straight up. He could do that, but it wore him out. He worked with one arm at a time and continued. There was no greater motivator than anger and frustration. He was going to get moving again. He tried to do a sit-up; not gonna happen. But he could lift his body a bit. He lifted his head also ...ah, much better than a few hours ago. So Harv started, invented and used his routine. From center to his left side; back to center then to his right side; back to center, lift his left leg, then his right leg; his left arm and then his right arm; finally to try a sit-up and then to lift his head. It was hard work, but he kept at it. He found himself getting tired and sore. This was the first of many unpleasant surprises that Harv would experience.

As weariness both mentally and physically overtook him, Harv slid into a deep nap. He was awakened by someone in a uniform bringing him a tray that fit over the bed and some food. He found himself excited about the food. As the man adjusted the tray, food, utensils, and water, another brought a

TV on a rolling cart, plugged it into the cable and socket, and handed Harv the remote.

Not being able to sit up by himself, he asked the man who delivered the food to raise the bed so he could eat. The man said, "I'm Jason, an Orderly here, Mr. England. We're glad to see you finally awake and with us." He proceeded to show Harvey how to use the controls for his bed and raised him to a sitting position that allowed him to eat and watch the TV. Jason said, "When you're done with dinner or need anything, just punch the 'call button' right here on the TV remote" before he left the room. Harv turned on the television and began to eat his lukewarm dinner. He realized as he ate, just how hungry he was. The food was just OK, but he ate quickly and hungrily.

Once he had consumed most of his meal, he began paying attention to the news on the TV. The coverage was filled with reporting and commentary on this thing called the Coronavirus; some called it the COVID or COVID-19. What the heck was that? As he listened, he wondered why he had never heard of it. It seemed to be everyone across the U.S. was consumed by it! He thought that might explain why everyone was wearing masks ...or were they afraid of catching something from him?

He thought about all the questions he had.

When he finished his dinner, he punched the "call" button. A few minutes later Jason came into the room to get his tray and dishes. Harvey had the presence of mind to ask, "When you have a moment, would you please get me a notebook and pen or pencil? Also, I could use another desert." Jason responded with a nod and a chuckle saying, "I'll be back in a few."

Jason returned in about 20 minutes with another peach cobbler and a new spiral notebook and both and pen and pencil. Harvey preferred a pencil (he was an engineer). Harv enjoyed the second desert and thanked Jason for it and the notebook and writing implements.

Once Jason had left the room, Harv just thought about all the questions he must ask. He thought about asking anyone who happened to come by. Harv had met Jason and he knew there would be a night nurse or aid and perhaps other orderlies. Harv did not know them and still felt very odd about his circumstances. He had only become awake and aware earlier today and was not one to immediately trust just anyone, especially that Culpepper guy. He decided Brenda would be his best choice for now.

He then started to write down the questions which he could think:

"What day and date is it?"

"Exactly how long have I been here?"

"What hospital was I in prior?"

"When did I go to the hospital?"

"Did I take myself? If not who took me?"

"How long was I in the hospital?"

"Who is taking care of my bills? How?"

"Did anyone bring any of my clothes?"

"What is this Coronavirus thing? How about COVID-19?"

"Is the U.S. shut down?"

"What else should I know about?"

Now It Begins!

After thinking about all the questions to which he needed answers; Harv began his exercise routine. He started by lifting his head, 5 repetitions, each better than the one before. He could almost hit his chest with his chin, but it stretched and hurt. Now he rolled his whole body up onto his left side, then back to the center on his back, then onto his right side, and finally back to the center on his back. He did 5 reps of those. Then he lifted his right leg, knees bent and held it 5 seconds, let it down, and lifted his left leg for the same time. Another 5 reps. Finally, he did 5 reps lifting his right and left arms and holding them for 5 seconds. "Wow am I out of shape!" he exclaimed.

Being the self-disciplined man, that he was, every time he woke up throughout the night, Harv did his exercises. He had sore muscles but felt some level of accomplishment. Early in the morning, he could not remember how many times through the night that he had done "his exercises". Before people came to check on him, Harv had swung his legs over the side of the bed and managed to, using his arms, back and stomach muscles, reach a sitting up position. That wore him out and he knew he shouldn't dare stand up at this point. But knowing he could do some maneuvering himself was a great feeling! Harvey was tired and stiff by morning.

As things around the Wildstone began to hum and bustle, Harvey was hungry. He was hoping for a good breakfast and a chance to spend some good time with Brenda. He knew she had others to care for but really needed the time with her. The good news was that breakfast was good. He got scrambled eggs with cheese, a bagel with butter, and some fruit. It was just what he needed. The bad news was that Brenda was in a training session and would not be in until afternoon. But he watched TV and read the paper that was brought to him. The News Gazette gave him some information he needed immediately. It was May 26th, the Tuesday after Memorial Day weekend! It was still 2020 and the clock on the wall claimed the same time as the TV and it was now 9:32 a.m. In his mind, Harv said to himself, several times over, "I'm at Wildstone Senior Living Community in Champaign, IL and it is May 26th, 2020 at 9:32 a.m." He felt very strongly that he needed to be confident of that information.

Knowing that Brenda was going to be there in the afternoon, Harv did "his exercises" and was pooped. He'd only been conscious for a short time. He decided to take a nap and he was out like a light!

When Harv awoke at around 11:15 a.m., he turned on the TV and saw some Memorial Day clips from the past weekend. He remembered his military service and some of his experiences and felt a swell of pride. A passing thought flowed through his mind that of the U.S. population, only approximately 7 % were veterans. Harvey did not know where or when he heard that information but found that even if it were close to true, the number was way too low.

The anchorman was talking about the huge percentage of deaths from COVID that occurred in nursing homes and long-term care facilities. Harvey was bothered by that number and, in his mind, decided he needed to get out of here and back home as quickly as possible for his own good!

Jason came in with Harv's lunch and gave him an upbeat greeting. Harv thanked him and was pleased to receive his small salad, chicken breast, and jello. The jello was too rubbery to be eaten but Harv thought it would be a good toy.

Feeling better after something to eat, Harv did a few more repetitions of his 'exercise program'. It felt good to know that he could now do most of his movements much more easily; not easily enough, but it was still an improvement. Harv thought back to the half-marathon he had run last year for Veterans Day and thought it would be great if he could do it again next year.

Then to his happy surprise, Brenda was back. They exchanged greetings and Harvey asked if he could talk with her about the questions he had so that he could begin to understand things and move on. Brenda said she would come back later in the day, but she had a surprise for him. At that point, she told Harvey that a Physical Therapist (a P.T.) was coming by shortly to begin helping Harv get back into shape. As he expressed his gratitude for that, in walked the P.T. himself. Brenda introduced him as John Moran. He was a good-sized man appearing to be strong and conditioned. Harvey liked that because he wanted to feel secure with one who would be working with him. John seemed enthusiastic and said, "Nice to meet you, Harvey. Let's get started!"

Both Brenda, who had stayed around for a bit, and John were surprised by how agile Harv was and, while having little stamina, how strong he was. The first thing John did was help Harv move to a sitting position on the side of the bed. Because Harv had been practicing this move, he found it relatively doable. But, once he reached the sitting position, he was a bit dizzy. John told him that was common and to just wait a moment. Harv felt better in moments. Then came the first real test. John fastened a very wide belt around Harvey's waist which had grab loops on it so he could hold Harvey. He then asked Brenda to lower the bed until Harvey's feet were on the floor. Once there, John asked Harvey to stand up. While John, from the front, held the side loops on the support belt, Harvey tentatively stood slowly. Harv realized that he had little strength in his legs after five months in bed in both the hospital and Wildstone Senior Living Community. As he stood, he felt himself shaking a bit, but he was committed to the task. Harv took a couple of deep breaths once standing and began to step forward. John was not quite expecting that and said, "Where are we going?" Harvey said, "anywhere and as far as I can." Both John and Brenda made sure to tell Harv that anytime he left the room that he must be wearing a mask as they did, and they gave him a paper mask to wear. Brenda put a couple more in the drawer of his nightstand. Not wanting to stop Harv's momentum, John asked Brenda to grab a wheelchair that was in the hallway outside the room and to follow them. Very carefully, Harvey walked out the door into the hallway, turned right, and went toward the nurses' station at the front of the building. Having not seen this part of the home before Harv asked where the hallways went and how big the home was. Once at the nurses' station, Harv was really tired and getting too shaky for safety. He took a seat in the wheelchair and Brenda took him on back to the room. Both John and Brenda were impressed.

Once back in the room, John gave Harv a squeezy ball to exercise his hands and some weighty beanbags for Harv to hold while lifting his arms for exercise. After warning Harvey that he'd be back tomorrow, he left. Brenda told Harv she was impressed and that she had to do some rounds, but she'd be back later, and she left the room.

Harvey pondered upon what had happened. While he was pleased he was getting up and about, he realized he had little stamina and muscle tone. He wondered how long it would be before he could get the damn catheter out and begin to use the toilet instead of a bedpan and his catheter. Before taking a nap, he decided to do his exercise routine a couple of times, now adding lifting the bags with his arms and squeezing the ball with his hands. Harv then gladly slipped away for some rest.

At about 3:45 Brenda returned to Harvey's room as she had promised. Harv was pleased and looking forward to getting some answers and catching himself up. Brenda sat down in the chair next to the bed and told Harv he could ask her anything.

Harvey first asked, "When did I go to the Hospital?" Brenda surprised him when she said, "It was December 19, 2019. It was the week before the students went on Christmas break. That's what my records show, anyway."

Harv was astonished. "That means I've been in the hospital and then here for over five months! I thought it was about three and a half months." Brenda explained that he was sent to Wildstone after a lengthy hospital stay. It was only once that he was not contagious and that they felt there was little progress to be made that they send him on to Wildstone.

Harvey said, "You mean that I was not expected to make any 'progress'? What exactly does that mean? Come on Brenda, tell me!"

Brenda sighed, took a breath, and replied. "Harvey, I suppose there's no harm in telling you now that you're back with us that nobody; not the doctors, nurses, therapists, etc. thought you would survive. I used to come by your door and look in just hoping to see you there alive every day but thinking one day you won't be there anymore." A tear came to her eye. She went on, "Now that I've started to come to know you, I'm so pleased." She was full-on crying now. Harv did not know what to say. He tried to comfort her saying, "I hope those are happy tears because I'm thrilled to know you!" Brenda giggled a little, pulled a tissue from her pocket, and wiped away her "happy tears".

So, Harvey asked, "What hospital was I in for 5 or 6 weeks?" Brenda answered, "Carle Hospital". Harvey asked, "Do you know who my doctor was?" Brenda did not know so Harvey asked her to make a call and find out.

"So how did I get to Carle," Harv asked. Brenda told him that early the morning after his college presentation, the UPS driver had stopped by to bring a package of auto parts he had ordered and as the driver was in the breezeway, he looked in the window and saw Harvey on the floor. He called out for Mr. England but got no response so-called 911.

Harvey then asked, "Where are my clothes? I want to get out of this damn gown and into my own clothes." Brenda replied that he would have to wait until the catheter was out within a couple of days likely to wear regular clothes. She didn't tell him that she had no idea where his clothes were.

Finally, Harvey asked the obvious question, "Who is paying my bills? And how without my involvement?" This one caught Brenda in the dark. She said, "I have no idea how that's being done right now. Do you have someone with Power of Attorney or a lawyer who might be involved?" After a distinct, "No" from Harvey they both wondered about that. Brenda said it must be handled by the business office. "Probably your Medicare and Supplement is receiving the bills. I'd advise you to wait until you're more 'resilient' and have more information before you speak with them. They sometimes talk in circles over there."

Harvey laughed a little, but it caused him considerable concern that occupied his thoughts for a bit. He asked Brenda two more questions. First, he asked Brenda, "Please tell me more about this place. I've only seen my room and a bit of the hallway to the nurses' station."

To this, Harv got a much longer answer. Brenda said, "Wildstone Senior Living Community is the largest full-service nursing, assisted living, independent living and rehabilitation home in the area. It is part of a much larger group of homes throughout the Midwest. It is exceptionally large. On the far side of the property, we have a separate building for those with memory disorders, dementia, Alzheimer's, etc." She went on, "On the far side of this building we have an area for those who are suffering from the COVID-19. We're being incredibly careful because those who are aged and/or suffering from pre-existing conditions like asthma, diabetes, COPD, etc. are those who most easily succumb to this virus. There is an exceptionally large food service kitchen who prepare the meals and a lovely dining facility for those who can gather there to have really good meals. Because of the virus, not many people are going now. We then have this full-care facility where you are. It is obviously for those who can't live unassisted at all. On the other side of the property is an assisted living facility for those who can live on their own, but we provide cleaning and laundry services, meals, and transportation if necessary. There is also a beautiful area of independent living apartments for those who are largely self-sufficient. We're a big facility, Harvey."

"Do you always wear a mask?" Brenda said, "Normally not, but we're all required to wear them because of the virus.

As we told you earlier, whenever you can leave your room, you will be required to wear one too."

"Thanks, Brenda; you've been so helpful. Is there a brochure or anything with some information about Wildstone that I could read? Maybe with a map of the facility in it? Also, Brenda, please ask the admin to get several changes of my own clothes for me. I don't expect it will be long until I get rid of this catheter and bedpan."

Brenda said, "I don't think it will be long either. You seem determined. I'll check on it for you."

When she left, she wrote an email to Mr. Culpepper telling him of Harvey's rapid recovery and toughness. She also told him that Harvey wanted several changes of his own clothes and his cell phone. Brenda also expressed her pleasure in watching Harvey work toward his recovery and return to his home and life. Brenda also mentioned that Harvey asked about his bills and she told him to talk to the business office when he was better. She said that Harv's an extremely resilient man.

Later, she was very surprised to get called into Mr. Culpepper's office and was more surprised by what he would tell her!

Harvey Expands his Territory

As the week went on, Harvey was feeling well. He had made good strides both mentally and physically. Several times he had done his exercise routine and found himself being able to move about without pain or discomfort. His sense of balance was even much better. He studied more about COVID 19. It had taken more than 100,000 lives and nursing homes suffered the worst of it. Old folks who were in poor condition and who had heart problems, diabetes, breathing issues, and other troubles were at great risk. Plus, he learned that it was hard to isolate oneself in a nursing home. Even in a room with the door closed, the heating and air conditioning units often shared common ductwork that carried the disease throughout a facility. In fact, Harvey asked for some additional masks for himself. While he had no conditions, he was weak due to so many months in bed.

Harvey had also learned more about Wildstone Senior Living Community. He knew about it largely because he had in the past, driven by the facility many times. He also knew how he had been found and taken to Carle Hospital. He would have to thank the UPS driver. But Meningitis? How and where in the world did he catch that? Harvey's thoughts went to the students he had seen earlier in the day. Had they been exposed? He would have to call them. That brought to mind that Harvey needed his phone. He would request one, or that they would bring him his cell phone and charger from home. The keys were still in his pockets if they needed to get in!

After breakfast, John Moran, the P.T. showed up as promised. Today he focused on Harvey using a walker to help him walk safely and independently. Harv took to it like a bird on the wing. His improving strength and balance helped him to walk further and further without much restriction. His use of the weighted beanbags for his arms along with his own routine had caused his strength to improve exponentially. John led Harv back to his room, let him into bed, and then said, "This is the big test that will make your life so much better." Harvey looked slightly bewildered so John said, "If you can do this next exercise, we'll be able to get you off the catheter and bedpan."

That's all that Harvey needed to hear. John first asked Harv to sit up on the edge of the bed with his legs hanging over toward the floor. He reminded Him to wait a few moments to ensure his head was clear and there was no dizziness. Then John instructed him to reach over and pull the walker into position. Harvey experienced no problems with that. Then, finally, John, while poised close in case it didn't go well, told Harvey to hold onto the walker and lower himself to the floor in a standing position. They both were surprised how easily it went. Then it was up to Harvey to go to the bathroom. Once there, John coached Harv through turning around and using the safety bars around the toilet, to sit down on the toilet. Next came standing up to the walker, moving to the sink to wash, and then going back to bed. Harv did fine! He was excited. He also realized that getting back into bed was harder than it looked!

Once he was back in bed, he thanked John. "John, I appreciate you helping me. This will allow me to do so much more independently." But he asked John, "Will it be OK if I sit in the chair in my room rather than always return to the bed?" John told him without reservation that would be better for him and his recovery. Harvey felt like a new man!

Lunch was there at about 11:45 when Jason arrived. I was tasty, a chicken salad sandwich, a small salad with ranch dressing, and a small bag of chips. After lunch, Harv decided to take a short nap.

Soon, during the early afternoon, Brenda got a message at the nurses' station. It was odd. It was from the Chief Administrator's office asking her to call. Of course, she called right away. Charlene, Mr. Culpepper's administrator answered on the 3rd ring. Brenda thought it was an intentional control thing for Charlene because she always waited for the 3rd ring. "Mr. Culpepper's office, Charlene speaking," she answered even though she had call waiting and knew from whom the call came. Brenda ignored that and said, "Hi Charlene. I received a call from Mr. Culpepper and wanted to respond." Charlene asked Brenda to hold on. Within a moment Charlene was back on the line. "Mr. Culpepper needs to see you right at 8:30 a.m. tomorrow. Please don't be late." Brenda answered in the affirmative and wondered to herself, "What could this be?" Mr. Culpepper was certainly not the complimentary type and relatively few of the employees had ever been to his office. His job was certainly not small, but he liked to think of himself as equal to a CEO or a large hospital administrator. His ego was bigger than his responsibilities or his abilities. Brenda liked her job at Wildstone Senior Living Community and wanted to keep it. She decided she would stroke his ego while telling the truth. Her integrity was important to her.

Upon awakening from his after-lunch nap, Harv decided to do his workout routine. After a couple of repetitions, he relaxed, got up from the bed being incredibly careful as John had shown him, and moved into the chair by his bed. "Ahhhh," Harvey thought as he got comfortable. This was much better; better for reading, watching television, and even for short naps. Now all he needed is the catheter out, his own clothing, and a phone. He was reading the News Gazette when Brenda came in. Harvey immediately, after exchanging pleasantries, asked Brenda to get him a telephone. He also requested his cell phone and charger that were at his place. He told her he had the key in his pants pocket when he passed out so it should still be there.

Harvey was very anxious to speak with his new friends and to put a plan together to go home. It seemed to make sense to him. Harvey was getting excited about beginning to move about. He also wanted to tour the grounds of Wildstone.

Harv was feeling rather good when John came in for the afternoon P.T. session. However, John had a surprise for him. John told Harv, "Slip on your shoes and come with me. We're going for a walk to the P.T. room." Harvey, still in a good mood complied with John's request, and down the hallway, they went. While still using a walker, Harv felt extremely comfortable and experienced little weakness or soreness while walking the hallways with John. It was a bit of a distance and Harvey was able to ask John about the hallways and where they led. Harv kept a sharp mental note because he hoped that soon he would be walking these hallways independently.

As they entered the room, Harv made his mental inventory. It was quite a large room and had stationary bikes, treadmills, an elliptical machine, weight benches, free weights, and several other contraptions with which he was not familiar. He was looking forward to this. John first went to a mobile staircase. It was 8 steps high and had a stair landing at the top with handrails on both sides. It was quite wide to accommodate patients of all sizes and shapes. John said, "Harv, it's time for you to get used to going up and downstairs." Harv responded, "Let's go!" Harv immediately let go of the walker which was becoming less and less necessary and approached the stairs. "Ah, ah, ah," said John firmly. "We're going to do it with the walker first." Harv acquiesced and grabbed his walker. John instructed him to first lift the walker to the next step and then to step up to it. While Harv had no problem with it, he sensed the considerable weakness in his legs and knees. He went up the eight stairs to the "landing." John told him how to reverse his direction and process and to place the walker on the next lower step and then climb down to it. Again, there was a success but a bit slow due to Harv's natural weakness. Upon getting to the bottom, Harv cussed a blue steak that surprised John. Harv was "totally pissed off" at his lack of strength compared to his abilities to do running stair laps before his falling sick. He was mad at the disease, mad at himself, mad that he was in this place, mad he could not go home yet, mad at the catheter, and just generally mad and frustrated. This was the first time he had openly expressed his frustrations and lack of independence. He told John, "From now on I am an independent adult and will make my own decisions. I will decide if and when I will use the walker. I will decide when and where I will take a walk, I'll decide what I'll eat and where I'll go. I have money and I will order Chinese food, take a cab to the mall or a movie. I will oversee myself!"

John listened and inside said, "Oh boy" to himself. He first apologized to Harvey for putting him in the situation to be reminded of his limitations. Second, he very carefully and tactfully reminded Harvey that the COVID was a real threat and if he caught it, he very well might not survive. Third, he knew that it would not be long before Wildstone could no longer keep him here without his consent. In fact, he might be able to leave the center "AMA" (Against Medical Advice) even now. Harvey was becoming physically able, was mentally well, and very sharp. It would not be his best choice, but it was a choice.

After Harv's tirade, John realized Harv needed some independence. He walked with Harvey to his room, waited for Harvey to be seated. "Harv, I do understand your frustration. I going to do something to help you, but I will need your assurance that you will not overdo things and set yourself back." I'm going to complete our wellness form which tells nurses, orderlies, and therapists throughout Wildstone that you are cleared to walk around both inside the facilities and outside within the grounds of Wildstone except for the COVID unit. I will get you a copy that you must carry with you whenever you go roaming. Will that help?"

Harvey was thankful and a bit contrite. He told John he genuinely appreciated his help and rehab, he expressed some apologies for his outburst but also told John, whom he had entrusted, about his deep frustrations. John clearly understood. It was common to observe frustration with patients who had to rely on aides to do everything for them to include taking them to the bathroom and showering them. While Harv no longer needed that care in his opinion, his frustration made perfect sense.

Almost Ready

Today was a better day. Harv felt good, and Jason brought him a breakfast that Harv consumed in total. He was going to ask; not demand of Brenda that his catheter be removed and that he would receive his clothing. He was ready to get to independent roaming!

At 8:30 sharp, Brenda was in Anthony Culpepper's office. While it was similar in size to the offices of other executives like the Purchasing Manager, Finance Manager, Facilities Manager, and others, it was decorated in a much more "executive" fashion. There were paintings on the wall that were of Mr. Culpepper's specific tastes while other executives just took what was provided. He had a couple of small oriental-style rugs on the floors and rather than the door sign state "Chief Administrator" it had his full name in large letters above the title. It was clear that Anthony was a bit if not mostly narcissistic. She had arrived earlier and was kept waiting, Brenda thought, as a control measure. Mr. Culpepper always had to have the upper hand.

Rather than come out to the waiting area himself, at about 8:35 he buzzed the secretary and asked her to bring Brenda back.

As Brenda entered his office, he stood but did not offer his hand, standard during these days of COVID. He motioned to her to take a seat. He said, "Ms. Williams, please tell me how Mr. England is doing. He's an unusual case due to his survival, and I take an interest in him."

Brenda was initially pleased with his question, thinking that mostly one would get invited to Mr. Culpepper's office to either receive admonishment or specific instructions for something. "Mr. England is doing so well. He is excellent with his Physical Therapy, and he is getting stronger by the day, he's reading voraciously and wants to learn more about Wildstone. In fact, as you know from my note, Mr. Culpepper, he has asked for some of his clothes and his cell phone and charger. He said his keys are in the pants he was wearing when he was initially brought in the hospital. I have no authority to get them for him, but I'm sure you can do so, please. I know it would make him happy."

In a very condescending tone, the Chief Administrator replied, "It's good that he is making good strides as it is our jobs to help our patients. Let us be careful about giving him too much latitude too soon, though. I will consider his requests. It is important to be positive with him, but let's not lose control of him at this point. Do you understand me, Brenda?" She said, "Not completely, no." He replied, "Well, let's get specific. You are not to be too flattering in his progress and do not promise or imply anything. In other words, he will wear a hospital gown as long as I say so. He will remain under our; 'err my control. Do you clearly understand Brenda?"

"Wow," said Brenda to herself. "Yes, I understand." He looked at her and said, "I understand Mr. Culpepper." She said back to him, "Yeah; I've got it." She stood and began to make her exit and watched him scowl at her. "Shove it," she thought and left.

As Brenda walked down the long hallway, she wondered what about Harv interested Culpepper so much. Was Harvey a past enemy? What could the reason be? Harv was such a fine man, and as his progress continued, he was going to become completely independent and move home soon. It pleased her to know that he would get his life back!

Brenda, being suspicious, went promptly to Harvey's room. He was sitting in his chair, finishing his breakfast and reading about Wildstone Senior Living Center from the very inclusive and complete brochure along with many picturesque and flattering photos of people enjoying themselves. He saw Brenda and asked her to sit with him. He said, "Brenda, thanks for getting this brochure for me. It's really useful." He held up his "Wellness Form" that gave him much more freedom. "I feel great about this. It gives me hope."

Brenda couldn't help herself and asked, "Have you and Mr. Culpepper had any conversations?" Harvey quickly recalled how he disliked the man and how Harv had told the "Chief Administrator" that he did not work for him and that he was very personally capable. Brenda knew immediately why Anthony Culpepper was working to exert control, the snake. But she only knew a small part of things. Even though Mr. Culpepper had given directions to Brenda, after seeing Harv's Wellness Form signed off, she said, "Harvey congratulations on the Wellness Form. That is a real step toward independence and healing. Please wait for me here, and I'll be back."

Brenda then went off to find the clothes Harvey had when he was at the hospital. It surprised her, but his belongings came with him from the hospital to Wildstone. They were in a large kraft paper bag with his name on it. She opened the bag to see the handsome business-casual attire that Harv had worn for the college presentation. She sent them down to the laundry and had them all laundered and ironed for him. She checked the pockets, and Harvey's keys were still there as he had said. She took them from his pants pocket and slipped them into her bag. She also took his wallet to return to him. A nice Movado sports watch was also in the pocket, and that went along with Brenda. The laundry said Harv's clothes would be ready by 4:00 p.m. Brenda decided not to tell him but surprise him with the clothes and personal items. She returned to see Harvey still reading in his chair. She said, "Thanks for waiting for me. I was just arranging for something." She then handed Harvey a couple of excellent cloth face masks. He had been using disposable paper masks when he left his room before this, but they were a pain and not too comfortable. "Harv, you must wear one of these anytime you are outside of your room, just like you have worn the paper masks. These will be more comfortable, and I can get them regularly washed for you." Harvey also knew he had several more paper masks he could use if necessary. "The biggest issue for you lately has been your catheter," Brenda affirmed. "I will be back later this afternoon to remove it. You may say

Hooray if you wish." With a huge smile, Harvey said, "Hooray" loudly! Then Brenda went on to say that now that Harv was independent, his room classification would no longer be full nursing care, but "assisted living" meaning meals, cleaning services and other items, as necessary. It would mean a lot more independence and lower cost.

Harv thanked Brenda, who then turned to leave to see her other patients. Harvey interrupted her exit as asked, "Is there a library or a place I can use a computer?" Brenda smiled and said anytime in the "Resource Room. It is on your map. You won't have to wait to use a computer because so many of our residents don't have them or use them." Harv commented that she was a wealth of information as she left.

Brenda smiled to herself as she realized that Harvey, who fell sick over five months ago and had significant muscle atrophy, was coming back like a star athlete. She couldn't imagine him living long in a nursing care facility. He was to be admired. "Yes, I like him. He's no pushover, but he's polite and well-spoken." she thought.

It was about 4:15 p.m. when Brenda picked up Harvey's clothes that he was wearing at the time of admission, at the laundry. They looked great. Brenda took them and headed right away to Harvey's room. Just before she entered the room, she put Harv's wallet, watch and keys in the bag. She went into Harv's room and handed him the bag. He asked what it was and then looked in. Harv was elated! He thanked Brenda repeatedly. When he looked through his wallet, he looked at Brenda and asked if there was a safe that residents could use. She said there was not, but she stepped out briefly and brought a padlock and keys to Harvey that would fit a small closet in the room. Again, he thanked her. Harv had well over $1,500.00 cash in his wallet and didn't want to leave it for someone to take. All his credit cards and bank cards were also in his wallet. Even more notable were a couple of photographs of Margaret! He wanted to protect his wallet! He was also pleased to have his watch.

Harv then went into the bathroom with his clothes, forgetting his walker on the way. As he prepared to put his clothes on, Brenda knocked on the door. "Aren't you forgetting something important?" she said. Harvey realized he still had the catheter in and came quickly from the bathroom ready to have it removed. Brenda explained that it would be quite uncomfortable. She also told him that after its removal, the muscles that prevented him from "leaking" after urinating would take time to regain their abilities. Harvey clenched his teeth as it was removed. It hurt! There was a trace amount of blood, but he felt immediately better. Brenda gave him some pads to use in his underwear until there were no more leaks. Now, as he donned his garments, he felt immediately more comfortable and presentable. He had lost some weight and particularly muscle tone over the last five months, so they did not fit him as well as they had, but it was a far sight better than the gown! He emerged from the bathroom to watch Brenda's eyes light up. Harvey was very handsome, and one would not have guessed that he had any health needs to see him in his clothes. They were fine labels, excellent colors and looked great on him. He sat down and put on his shoes. Harvey felt terrific.

"You look great," Brenda said. "Thanks," said Harv. "When do you think you can get me my other clothes?" Brenda told Harvey she simply didn't know based on Mr. Culpepper's answers. Harvey thought for a moment and said, "You've seen my taste in clothes and colors. If I give you the cash will you go buy me socks, underwear, another 2 or 3 pairs of pants, 3 or 4 shirts and a jacket?" Brenda could not decline. Harvey gave her $275 from his wallet and thanked her.

Because it was 4:45 p.m. by this time, even though Harvey was aching to take a walk around the facility, he knew he should start tomorrow when he had all day apart from P.T. It would also give him some time to experience life without a catheter! He smiled as he sat down to memorize the facility map. Tomorrow was going to be a great adventure!

An Important Meeting

The next morning, Anthony Culpepper sat across the desk from Charles Bilford as they talked. Mr. Bilford was a long term "friend" of Culpepper's who had grown up with him in the same neighborhood and an attorney for Wildstone as well as a member of the Board of Directors.

Mr. Culpepper was saying, "Charlie, this matter with Mr. England cannot blow up in our faces in any way! He wants his clothes and cell phone, and soon he'll be asking for his money and to go home! He's just received his completed P.T. card and is building his strength back. The two questions are, "Can we get back his home and all furnishings and belongings?" and "Have we transferred his investments? Can we get them back without calling attention to ourselves?"

Mr. Bilford replied, "This is all your fault, Tony. You were cocksure that England would die very soon and had the doctors all agreeing with you. His house is sold, the new owners love it, and the proceeds are split between Wildstone and us, as not to raise suspicion, and his investments have been handled the same way. As you know full well, we sold his furnishings and other assets except for the specific ones we held onto. We can't get them back. And, if we pay him back from the Wildstone accounts, the funds will put Wildstone in the red, and we'll have auditors down our backs and likely lawsuits that we won't win. We simply have to try to keep him in a "needy" state if you know what I mean."

"So, exactly how do we do that?" Culpepper replied. "And do we have to do it until he actually dies? He was the right person for us to choose. He had a nice, upscale condo paid for, beautiful furnishings, that mustang and a big bank account from the sale of his business, savings, and oil company pension. He has no immediate family to meddle, and he was supposed to die soon. How could we know he'd live?"

"I don't have the answers, but Tony, you've come up with many nefarious ideas before. Maybe you could use medications to dull him even awareness-wise and physically. But I can guarantee you that without something, it won't be long before we are dragged into court with lots of explaining to do, and you'll lose your job, I'll be disbarred, and we'll both go to jail for a long time. You'd better do something. I'm very concerned about this turn of events. We'd better talk often.

Do not do anything without speaking with me! If he were to have died as he was supposed to, our plan would have worked beautifully. But be very careful. I, for one, will not agree to anything that could bring a murder charge... and you don't want that either!"

As they closed the conversation, Charlie reminded Tony that they should still meet at Wildstone weekly and have lunch together regularly because that had been their habit. Changing their known routine would raise suspicion.

"Let's talk soon, and let me know what your ideas are Tony," Bilford said. "Yeah, I get it," said Culpepper. And the meeting was over.

Charlene buzzed Mr. Culpepper after Mr. Bilford had left. "I have some appointment requests for you," she said. Mr. Culpepper told her to cancel the afternoon's appointments because he had some priority issues to think about.

Anthony Culpepper, in significant distress, put his "thinking cap" on!

Out and About

It was an exciting morning for Harvey England. For the first time, he woke up, showered, and got ready for the day without any assistance. He was dressed in his good clothes and armed with a map of the facility and mask he took off right after breakfast. Jason had cheerfully brought his breakfast because the common dining facility was off-limits because of the COVID-19 outbreak. As Jason saw Harvey looking good and ready, he had positively greeted him. "So, you got a big day today?" Jason asked. Harvey replied that he was going to take a long walk around the facility. Jason advised him to see the assisted and independent living facility because of the beautiful independent apartments, patios, and landscaping. So Harv decided to do just that!

Harv walked as far as the nurses' station and then turned left toward the main entrance. He was feeling energetic but had taken his walker because he had not walked so far in months. The main entrance was obvious. It was somewhat grand with high ceilings, beautiful paneling and artwork with furniture resembling a fine hotel lobby. He looked toward the entrance and exits with three large, double-doors and chose to exit to the far right, closest to the independent and assisted living areas. Out the door, he went, and Harv experienced an emotional moment as he realized he had not been outside a medical facility on his own in five months!

He took the sidewalk to the right as he recalled his memorized instructions from the map. Deciding to go the farthest point first and then work his way back, Harv went all the way to the buildings for independent living apartments. It was a pretty walk, he noted. What he noticed along the way based on the signage was that "assisted living care" was available in all the areas if one needed the extra level of care. Harv was a bit tired after 20 minutes or so chose to sit on one of the many benches along the lovely, paved brick path. "What a good day," he thought. As he surveyed his surroundings, a voice off to his left side said, "You tired, lost, lonely or just getting away?" Looking in the direction of the voice, he saw a sort of rugged and stocky man sitting on a ground floor, outdoor patio evidently part of his apartment. Harv yelled back, "I don't know …I'm old, and I forgot!" The other gentlemen started laughing and said, "Well, I don't want to be responsible for getting you lost. Come over here and sit with me!"

Harv smiled. It was nice to see someone here with a good sense of humor. He went over to the man via a well-worn path and extended his hand. "Harvey England," he said. "Many just call me Harv." His host said, "Have a seat Harv. It's good to have some company. My name's Walt Schell. Let's talk. Want a cup of coffee?" Harvey asked, "If it's good, sure. If it's not, no thanks." Walt stood and told Harv to sit tight. In a moment he was back with the extra cup.

As they drank coffee, they got to know one another. Walt learned that Harv had been extremely ill, not expected to make it but had surprisingly rebounded and was just now becoming more physically and mentally fit. He was wondering what his future would hold. Harv learned that Walt's wife, Debbie had been exceptionally ill and to get her the care she needed, Walt had given all their assets to Wildstone to pay for the small but nice apartment. After his wife had died, even though Walt had no impairments, he had to continue to live at Wildstone because he had no other assets to move out, buy furniture, a car, etc. But Walt was happy, and his apartment was excellent. They learned that they were both Vietnam Veterans and were both formidable characters. Well, at least Harv would resume that status as he continued to heal.

Walt and Harvey wiled away a couple of hours enjoying one another's company. Finally, Harv told Walt that he wanted to see the rest of the complex before going back to his room with the promise of getting together again soon. Walt suggested that because of the COVID his meals were good and delivered to his apartment, maybe they could request Harv's meal be delivered to Walt's place too, and they could have dinner. Walt made a note of telling Harv, "I have wine here!" Harv said, "Deal is done," and walked off.

As Harvey "toured" the rest of the buildings, he noted how beautifully it was maintained and the landscaping was nice. He was surprised that there were not more people outside using the tennis courts, shuffleboard, walking trails and other facilities.

When he returned to his room, it was about 1:00. He was surprisingly tired but also realized he had walked quite a distance. He sat down, hoping he wasn't too late to get some lunch. Just about that time, Jason appeared and stated that he had saved some lunch for Harv. "Good deal," Harv thought and heartily ate the excellent salad, ham, and pineapple with a pudding dessert.

He was ready to take a brief nap when Brenda Williams arrived. She had some packages. She put them on Harv's bed and opened them. There was a nice pair of blue jeans, a pair of khakis, some beige canvas slacks and four very nice shirts. She also produced two 4-packs of underwear and ten pairs of socks. She threw in a business-casual brown belt and a Columbia navy-blue jacket. Harvey was so delighted. He now felt that he could look good, be acceptable anywhere he went and be more like "himself" before the illness. He went to hug Brenda with big thanks. She initially backed off and said I can't because of the COVID. After a short second thought, she approached Harvey and they bear-hugged.

Brenda then tried to give Harv his $16.50 in change. Harv refused. They exchanged frustrated looks before they both laughed. Brenda, though, could not help herself. She told Harv she needed to speak with him quietly and seriously. Intrigued, Harvey pursued the conversation. Brenda confided in Harvey that she was concerned about him. She expressed to him that she felt that Anthony Culpepper had been overly worried about the interactions between Brenda and Harvey, and Culpepper's assertion of "control aggravated it." She was also profoundly concerned that Harvey's request for his cell phone and wardrobe was not denied, but that nothing had been done. She didn't know why but there was a feeling that something underhanded was going on. She told Harv to watch his back and be careful about who he talked to and confided in.

Harv was confounded, miffed, and also very upset by Brenda's news. He trusted her, and she had no reason to fabricate this story. He would, indeed, be careful, listen and heighten his awareness. Harv did not like this Culpepper and would not hesitate to stand up to him. Harvey had run a highly successful company and regularly worked with people way above Culpepper's pay grade. Because he was not physically in excellent shape yet and Brenda's thoughts were the only suspicion at this point, he felt the best approach was to take notes, listen and move forward toward his return home.

He laid back in his chair, closed his eyes and went through what he felt, what he thought, what he saw and heard and what he knew. He needed to sort this out. He opened his eyes, reached for his notebook and pencil, and began to write. Taking notes helped him to consider the facts.

Learning about the Problem

Harvey was eating breakfast when the landline phone in his room rang. It was the first time he had heard it since it was installed after he "woke up". He answered it, "Harv England." The voice on the other end was familiar. "Harv; this is Walt Schell. Why don't you walk over here about 4:30 this afternoon? We'll drink some wine, talk some and I can even introduce you to my great neighbor, Tory. What d'ya say?"

Harv immediately answered, "Sounds a whole lot better than watching TV and falling asleep too early. I'll be there. And, Walt, thanks." He felt as if he had a personal friend. Just how much would soon be determined.

After breakfast, he had an idea. Harv had, before his illness, taken an active role in keeping up with and managing his investment accounts. He decided he would check on them and with his bank. He knew things would feel better. But he didn't have his notebook with all of his data. It had been on his desk in the condo. "Wait," he thought. "I'll go to the small library and use a computer."

Harv decided to take his notebook and pencil with him and away he went to the library. He noticed he did not require a walker along the way. He took it anyway because he didn't want to anger John, but he'd leave it in the room tonight when he went to Walt's.

Once in the library, he sat down at the PC and thought of the inquiries he needed to make. Because Harv and run a significant business and company, and he was an engineer, he was a savvy computer user. His list included:

Check his investment account balances

Check his bank account balances

Check on his auto payments for utilities, cable, etc.

He first googled Jensen Securities, who handled his investments, wrote down their phone number and did the same for Veterans' Bank. He first made the call to Jensen Securities. As they answered, he asked for Andrea, who was his excellent investment advisor. "She'll be with you in a moment, sir," said the receptionist. While he waited, Harv got his pencil and pad ready."

"Andrea Carlin, may I help you?" she answered. "Hi Andrea, it's Harvey England."

"Oh my gosh, Harvey! It's been so long! Are you all right? I have so many questions for you!" Harv answered, "As do I of you, Andrea. First, I'm OK and getting better every day. To make a long story short, I fell gravely ill approximately five months ago, was in the hospital for almost two months, and then was transferred to Wildstone with little hope for survival. But I beat the odds, and now I'm working on regaining my strength and independence."

Andrea replied, "Oh Harvey, I had been informed you were extremely ill and would likely not make it. I'm so pleased you're on the mend!" "So how did you find out?" asked Harvey. Andrea responded, "I hadn't talked to you in weeks which was highly unusual. Then I received the Power of Attorney forms and realized that you must have been ill to give up your control of your investments."

Harvey was immediately flustered and thoroughly pissed! "I didn't give up anything," he said. "I never signed a Power of Attorney. Who did the form come from and who got my power of attorney?" Andrea said, "Some attorney with Bilson & Associates, PLC. I don't remember the name, but I'll find out for you and call you back later. It may be tomorrow." Harvey then asked, "So, Andrea, how much do I still have in the account?" Andrea started stumbling and was aghast as she said, "Harv, it's all gone. $853,550.00 was transferred out of your account into an escrow somewhere else. There's none left!" Harvey felt faint. His entire life's work and savings were gone. He was reticent. "Harvey, are you there? Are you all right?" Andrea asked. Harvey replied, "Of course I'm not all right. I will need to know exactly who stole my money and where it is currently. How would you feel if someone took all your money?"

What made this whole situation worse was that due to privacy laws, once the money had been transferred out of his account, Andrea could not give him any of that information. It would require a court order. She felt so unbelievably awful as she explained it to Harvey. At this point, Harvey was raging! It was made even worse when Andrea said that Harv would have to know and be able to prove some sort of wrongdoing to get such an order. It would be an unpleasant task. Harvey hung up with Andrea, not hating her but the situation. He knew he was in trouble and felt that Culpepper had something to do with it. And he was going to find out! Heads would roll!

The next call Harv made was to Veterans' Bank. He was directed to a senior Teller who told him he couldn't give him the answers to his questions over the phone. Harv demanded to speak with the manager. When Neil Goldman, the manager answered, Harv, identified himself. Neil was as surprised as Andrea had been to hear from him.

"Harv, I heard you were very ill! It's been months. I'm glad you're OK." Harvey told him, "There's something terrible going on, Neil. I just found out that Jensen Securities had a Power of Attorney, supposedly signed by me, and whoever it was, cleaned out my investments. I need to find out about my checking and savings accounts at Veterans' Bank." Neil responded much as Andrea had. He went on to tell Harvey that a Power of Attorney had allowed his checking and savings accounts to be transferred to some sort of escrow for a total of $275,000.00. He had been told it was for Harvey's support.

Now there was no question that a scheme had been instigated against Harvey, but he would have to prove it first. "As Harv talked with him, Neil came up with an idea. "Harv, they took everything under your name as the title. But remember the original account we set up for the sale of your business? We still have the original account in the name of England Projects Closing. It was not transferred because your name wasn't on the account title. You are the only signatory. It has the initial down payment still in the account for $173,000.00 and change. There's some interest accrued over the four years also. I can get you that amount." Harvey said, "Neil, we must keep that account a secret. Will my bank card work to get cash? They've taken everything. I'm terrified. I haven't even checked on my house yet. That's next." Neil said, "Your current bank card won't work for this account. I can send you one in the mail. What's your address?" Harvey thought for a moment and asked if he could have Brenda Williams pick it up. Neil said, "Sure. But let's have her ask specifically for me, and she'll have to show me I.D. Can we use the same password?" Harv said, "No. Change it to Gotcha20." Neil agreed. Now the chase would start.

Harvey felt a little better simply because he had some funds. But he wondered what has been done with his pension and social security payments? This situation required an outstanding investigator who could keep his mouth shut. Harv was ready to rumble. He also decided that he must get into shape quickly and surely. Tomorrow he would start. He also decided that he would share the story with Walt tonight. Brenda knew something was up, but Harv didn't want to put her job in jeopardy so he would limit what she knew. He needed to think!

After considerable thought, Harvey went back to his room. He did not eat lunch because this morning's revelations had stolen his appetite. Harv was so angry, befuddled and a bit depressed because of the loss of his investments, checking and savings accounts; they were what would provide for his "good life" once he went home. Between his Social Security, Brown & Root pension, and the profit-sharing from England Projects, coupled with his investments and savings, he had a good thing going. Right now, he didn't even know if he had a home. Harvey didn't know yet but felt that Walt would help him. Harv wanted to kick some butt, and knew he'd have to get into shape; this would be a good motivator. He made one more call to the accountant at England Projects.

"Hi Deb, it's Harv," he said into the phone. Deb was beside herself, and she told Harv that everybody missed him, worried about his health, and wondered how he was doing. Harv asked, "How did you find out I was ill?" Deb responded that one of an employee's friends worked for Carle Hospital and let them know that the past company owner and founder was ill. After some catch-up conversation, Harv asked, "It's been over five months now. How is my account doing?" Deb made him feel much better when she told him that several major jobs had been paid and new contracts were coming in, so his current balance from profits over the last four years was a little over $450,000.00. She asked, "Do you still want me to maintain it as a private account in our bank or do you want to transfer it to yours?" Harv told her that something was going on and he didn't want anything to happen to the money, so he asked her to keep it in the private account. She obliged and asked him to stay in touch. As she closed, she said, "I'll let the leaders know you're OK. We've all been praying and hoping." Harv thanked her and told her that he knew that prayer worked. Then they ended the call. "At least I've still got a significant Stache that's hidden; now to get back what's mine!" Harv thought.

It was a bit early when he showed up at Walt's apartment. Harv left the walker in his room and strolled independently to Walt's place. What he did not realize is that the upheaval and aggravation in his life this afternoon caused him to walk at a pace considerably faster than in previous days. Harv went up to the patio door and knocked because he didn't know the apartment number from the inside hallway. Walt came and smiled broadly. "You're early new friend. It must be that you're thirsty." Harv affirmed that and told Walt he had a sad story to tell and wanted to share it with him. Once the Cabernet was poured, they sat down, and Harv began to tell him the news. Walt was stunned but understanding. He stated that he also hated Anthony Culpepper and was a bit surprised that he might be involved in Harv's situation.

At that point, Walt made a suggestion. "I have another friend joining us tonight. You will enjoy her. Her name is Tory Randall, and she is wonderful. She graduated with her undergrad from Wabash College in Journalism and got a full ride to Columbia for her MBA. She worked for several newspapers over her career with the final ten years as the Editor for the Boston Globe. Tory is quiet but powerful. She can and will help us." Harvey interjected, "Us? Did you say us?" Walt smiled and said, "Absolutely friend. I've never been known to back down from a challenge, Harv. I'm with you all the way! Hoorah! This could be the most exciting thing that could happen to me. And Harv... we will fix this!"

Harvey felt better now. He had an ally and maybe, partners. As they continued to drink wine and talk more deeply now, Walt went more in-depth about himself. He told Harv he had gone to Auburn University, had continued his enjoyment of sky diving and received his Industrial Engineering degree, all after spending four years in the Navy during Vietnam. He was in a landing party. He had married Debbie when he got out and finished his career with the state's DOT. "When Debbie became so sick, well, you know the rest of the story since," said Walt. Harvey told Walt that he felt the need to get back into shape considering they had a challenging task ahead and Walt agreed to join him.

The doorbell rang, and Walt went off through the apartment to get the door. When he opened the door, Harv saw that it was apartment number 4G. He also saw the impeccably dressed and attractive woman in a wheelchair. Walt called him in and introduced her as his neighbor, Tory Randall. "How nice to meet you," she said. "I noticed you here on Walt's patio earlier but didn't interrupt." Tory came on in and started drinking wine with them. She was delightful and exceptionally articulate. Harv thought that it must have come from her years in journalism... speaking and writing correctly. Tory was very different. She dressed and spoke as if she were from high society, but her sense of humor and practical understanding of life itself made her one of them. It turned out that Tory had grown up on a farm east of Cleveland, Ohio and was as hardworking and normal as could be. She was some years younger than Harv but had been disabled in a bad car accident after receiving her MBA. Tory was able, using a walker, to get dressed, work in the kitchen, get in and out of bed and tend to her personal duties. This independent living apartment with meals supplied and a little daily help was perfect for her.

Dinner arrived at Walt's door. One of the "advantages" of the COVID-19 was that meals were delivered to the residents because the common dining area was closed. Walt had simply called the dining room and asked that the dinners for Harv and Tory be delivered to his apartment. Their meal of a salad, chicken breast with gravy, mashed potatoes, green beans, and a nice cherry pie was excellent. Wildstone often bragged about their food, and Harv had found it to be true.

Once dinner was completed, they moved to the small living room. Walt saw Harvey nod and took the lead. He said, "Tory, we have a situation that we never saw coming, and it's not good. I convinced Harv to count you into our small team that must deal with this. It could have massive consequences and affect us all. But I think your knowledge, brain and connections can help us. Confidentiality is especially important. If the others involved work here and they find out we are onto them, it could be dangerous and cause some of the employees we like to lose their jobs. We must be mum. Are you in?"

The Team's Assembled

You could see it in her face... Tory was not only in she was already committed to being part of the team. "The Team," Tory said. "It sounds good." Tory mentioned sarcastically with a smile that other than investigations into previous mayors, politicians, Watergate, Jimmy Hoffa's disappearance and other such high crimes and high-profile cases, she had no experience. Her "tongue-in-cheek" references were an excellent way for her to let them know that she was an experienced journalistic sleuth with useful contacts.

Harvey related the story to Tory and Walt with all the details known so far. He also let them know that he didn't know if he still had his condo, personal items, his mustang, clothing, Margaret's jewelry, artwork, Tiffany lamps, etc. As they thought about how to respond, Tory said, "If you think Culpepper's involved in this, let him hear the story that you are going to catch a cab to your condo to check on it, that you have the key and let's see what happens." Harv thought it over and said, "That's a great idea, and I think Brenda can mention something to Charlene and the rumor mill will work it out." But we need to be in touch; otherwise something terrible could happen."

Tory interjected that she thought that while giving them no proof, it would undoubtedly implicate Anthony Culpepper. In the meantime, she suggested that she contact Ted Hame, a famed investigative journalist she had known for years. She knew he was trustworthy and could uncover the real story over time. They all agreed, and she said she would keep them informed. She also suggested that someone, perhaps Walt was the best choice, should purchase three burn phones so that Walt, Tory and Harv could keep in touch confidentially. She made sense when she mentioned, "Remember that although we all have phones in our rooms, others can hear us when we take or make a call, and they may even be tapped. We need to be very, careful. Even though this is happening to one old senior citizen, sorry Harvey, there is enough money at stake that violence or "accidents" are a serious risk. I've heard of people being killed for much less than over a million dollars."

It's interesting that even as Harvey, Walt and Tory were assembled thinking through their strategy, Anthony Culpepper was getting more and more worried. His thoughts were that somehow heavily medicating Harvey might be a temporary solution. If England's memory failed and he was forgetful, much less a bit sloppy and unkempt, people would be much less likely to take him seriously. That, at a minimum, would buy him some time. Now, who could he get to prescribe such medication?

Harvey and Walt discussed meeting at the PT fitness room tomorrow a.m. at 9:00 to do their first workout. They agreed that stretches, some sit-ups, push-ups, light aerobics like jumping jacks and then some lighter weight free weights would be an excellent way to start. Tory laughed and told them to take some Advil afterwards. Harvey might call John to get some help.

Harv felt bad and a bit paranoid knowing that so much of his money was mostly gone, that the fraud had occurred while he was either in the hospital or since he has been at Wildstone, and he was still very anxious about his other belongings. Those emotions were becoming anger as they brewed. The Team had decided not to do anything else until they had their cell phones to communicate confidentially. Harvey wanted to get started but knew a day or two delay wouldn't hurt. He also felt that getting back into physical condition was very important. Otherwise, his lack of stamina and strength could get in the way.

His new friends had put together a team of people who could do a lot of good for Harvey, especially Tory. Her knowledge of people, sources of information and investigative processes were brilliant. Harv was very sure that Anthony Culpepper, if he were the perpetrator, would certainly have underestimated this team... and he was right!

After a good dinner and meeting, Harv felt like he had people on his side. He hoped so!

As they parted, Walt and Harv confirmed their 9:00 a.m. workout in the morning as Tory chuckled. Harvey strolled back to his building and to his room. As he got ready for bed, he took off his clothes and hung them up. It was a bit odd. He noticed that the new clothes Brenda had obtained for him were hung differently than they had been before he left. What could somebody be looking for? Harv decided to lock his notebook and research in his lockable cabinet along with his watch, wallet and keys. He could not afford to lose any of that material. He laid awake in bed for a long while just realizing the amount of damage that had been done to his life as he knew it. But he was a fighter and would attack the problem with his great friends!

The next morning while Harv was eating breakfast, Tory was busy on the phone with Ted Hame. She caught her old friend, the investigative journalist, at the right moment. They spoke about Harv's situation. Tory was not too concerned about privacy in her own apartment. Tory mentioned to Ted that certainly he had heard about abuses throughout the country perpetrated on seniors, especially when they are under the "supervision" of others who may have access to their finances or property or who wanted to access them. Ted was exceptionally understanding because he loved Tory and enjoyed hearing from her with this request for help. But also, because Ted's own parents were in an assisted living facility and Tory's proposal reminded him of the negative possibilities for his own folks! Tory's story about Harv and the fact that something had happened to his wealth, raised the suspicions of both Tory and Ted. And it had happened since Harv was admitted to the hospital.

Ted said, "Tory, this is very interesting and should never happen. Can you imagine who would go to a hospital or any kind of home if this can happen? I'll get started right away.

My first step will be to learn more about this and get some statistics about such theft. I'll also ask some friends in both law and finance to find out more. After that, I'll investigate Wildstone and their staff. It's a good time for me to do this because I've just completed another assignment, and this will end up being a great story. My boss will be in for this. I'll speak to you by late this week." Ted then actually warned Tory, "Tory, you and your friends be careful. Those who do these kinds of things do not want to be found out. And, in your kind of facility, you are a captive audience, and it's easy to explain away accidents and even worse. Watch yourself." Tory confirmed that they would and said, "We are going to get burn phones for our confidential communications." Ted asked that he receive the phone number when she got hers. They both thanked each other, wished each other well with verbal hugs and signed off.

Tory sat for a time thinking about Ted's "warning". She wondered what kind of harm could happen to any of them if the perpetrators found out about their investigation. She thought of physical injury and realized that it was more unlikely because those who committed such acts would likely be found out, even though such things did happen. She also realized that Wildstone was a very upscale multi-level care facility that they would be exceptionally concerned about their reputation. As Tory thought this through, she eventually came to the same conclusion that Anthony Culpepper had reached. Some sort of medication, either legally prescribed or illicit, could control or certainly restrict any resident.

Tory made note that during their next "meeting" they needed to prepare for such an incident. They needed someone on the staff to give them information!

Getting Ready

Promptly at 9:00 a.m. that morning, Walt showed up at Harvey's room. He was dressed in shorts and a baggie T-shirt. Harv wore some shorts and a T-shirt borrowed from John. "Hey Dude," Walt said. "Nice digs" as he teased Harv on his single, closed-in room. "You should move more upscale!"

"Like outa here?" Harv replied. They both laughed. They then headed down to the "workout room/gym" where John met them. John was great as he showed them the individual pieces of equipment, taught them how to correctly use them and then talked about safety in the area. He showed them four different exercises and recommended that they do a maximum of four repetitions through the first week, and then see how they were doing. After telling them to turn out the lights when they were done, he bid them farewell and quipped, "It's an Advil night tonight!"

They both started with some stretches. With their arms out to the side and perpendicular to their bodies, they first slowly, with their legs apart and their feet planted, turned back to the left as far as was comfortable, and then to the right

91

for the same distance. They did each stretch six times. Next, starting in the same position, they reached down in the direction of their feet with the opposite arm as far as was comfortable. Walt made it to mid-shin level, but Harv touched his left foot with his right hand. But, as he returned to the upright position, he became a bit dizzy, and Walt helped to steady him. "Man, are we out of shape," said Walt; stimulating the expected comment from Harv, "speak for yourself, Chubby." Then the competition began; sensible, but competition, nonetheless. Once they stretched, then each did five pushups. They rolled over onto their backs and did five leg lifts for five seconds each. They were both pooped! Both of them then went to the free weights and spotted one another. Each of them started with five-pound dumbbells and did five curls with each arm and then five side lifts with each. Finally, with their arms out straight, they each did five squats. They took a couple of minutes rest sitting on a bench and did them again. By the fourth repetition, both were weak and sore.

Harvey complained, "While I'm still an old poop, a year ago I could do 30 pushups, curl 70 pounds and then run a half marathon. I'm a mess." Walt said humorously, "I can still do that today, but I don't want to discourage you, old man."

"Go pound salt ya old fart," was Harv's reply with a chuckle. "Do you think if we keep at this, it will get any better?" They both nodded and agreed that it would do them good.

From the workout room, they both retired to their places to shower and get dressed. Walt kidded Harv and asked for a ride home. Harv said, "I've got a red '65 Mustang that would make your mouth water." "Can't wait to see it," said Walt! "How about 3:00, my place with Tory for some drinks and talk?" Harvey said, "I'll be there if I can walk that far after this!" and they parted ways.

When he got back to his room, Brenda happened to at the nurses' station and came down to Harv's place. After both of them laughed at Walt and Harvey's feeble athletic attempts, she asked how he was doing. Brenda then handed Harv the bankcard she had picked up from Neil at Veterans' Bank. She told him to please be careful with it and keep it under guard. She said, "Things are happening here that cause me to have questions." Harvey asked her if she would step outside to the courtyard with him. She questioningly agreed, and they walked down the hallway and out of the building. Brenda was confused and somewhat concerned.

"Brenda," said Harv, "I want to trust you with deep, deep confidence. I believe that you'll understand that to share this with anyone, I mean anyone, could throw my life into a worse disaster than it is. Can I trust you?" Brenda committed to Harv's trust.

Harvey told her of the story. "As you know, over five months ago I was hospitalized …you know more of that history than I do. Then I was transferred here where you cared for me and still are. Since I have awakened, and you gave me my wallet with my original clothes, I have called my investment house and Veterans' Bank to find that a forged Power of Attorney was used to take all of my considerable wealth and investments." Brenda interjected, "But the bankcard I just picked up …" Harv responded, "I did have an account that was not identified by my name so, thank God, I still have some money left. I still don't know about my house or other belongings. I need to find out. Brenda, I need to be able to trust you. Someone has stolen my assets, and I need them back."

Brenda said, "I knew something was up when I asked for your clothes and cell phone. I told Mr. Culpepper and received no response other than he would determine when and what you would receive. I felt that was mean and odd for him to say when he is supposed to be helping people. Oh, Harv, I'm so sorry. I will do what I can to help you."

"First of all, Brenda, being quiet, is the best thing. Tell nobody; friends, relatives, others here, nobody! I will ask you for something. I'm trying to test the waters. Please casually mention to Charlene that I'm planning on bringing my house keys and taking a taxi ride home to check on my house next week. She will likely tell Mr. Culpepper, and then we'll see how he responds. In the meantime, please find me any old key that looks like a house key and we'll put a tag on it that says, "England House". I will leave it in the nightstand drawer. We'll see what happens to it while I'm out of the room over the next week."

Brenda said, "That's perfect. I think it will get results. I only wish we had a camera in the room." Both agreed that they might think about that. "Brenda, one other slight concern. Last night when I was getting ready for bed, I noticed that my new clothes in the closet were moved around from where I had originally hung them. Any ideas of who might have come into my room to look? Are there any people on the floor, nurses or otherwise who you wouldn't trust with your things?" Brenda said that everyone she knew was utterly trustworthy except that the admin office could send over people to "review and inspect" peoples' rooms and the facility. They were supposed to sign in at the nurses' station. She would check and see who was here.

Then Harv asked her to please get him some athletic shorts, T-shirts, white socks, and tennis shoes for his "workout" sessions. She chucked and agreed. Harvey gave her some cash, and off she went.

Harvey closed and locked his room door at least to ensure his privacy while he was in the room. He knew the nurses, some orderlies and food service people had master keys but would rarely use them when the rooms were occupied. Harv took a nice hot shower, groomed, and got ready for the day. He had a lot to think about until he gathered with Walt and Tory. They were such great people. He wondered to himself as he had many times, how could he end up in such a situation?

At about 2:45, feeling clean and rested, Harvey set off for Walt's place. He was quite sore and stiff from this morning's first workout session but knew that he would work past the soreness over time. He made sure he stopped at the nurses' station to give them a greeting and let them know he would be gone until after dinner. He wanted to find out who was going into his room when he wasn't there. Harv had checked to make sure his things were locked up, and he had his notebook and wallet with him. Then he made his way to Walt's.

He was right on time and noticed that the walk was quick, and he felt great. His physical prowess was returning; slowly but returning. He went inside the building, went to 4G, and knocked. Walt answered, and as he opened the door, a "Hold the Door!" was heard as Tory came down the hallway. Both Walt and Harv smiled broadly as Tory zoomed toward the door. As they entered, they saw what Walt had prepared for them. He had a simple relish tray, some cheese and crackers, and the wine ready for them.   Both Tory and Harv spontaneously applauded, and Walt took a gracious and corny bow. They partook of the snacks and wine and settled down at the table for some very pertinent discussion.

The Current Situation

After some routine courtesies with Harv and Walt asking one another about their level of soreness after their first morning workout with the necessary sarcasm, they began to catch up in earnest. First, Tory spoke with them about her conversation with Ted Hame and his willingness and even interest to pursue their situation, or actually, Harvey's situation. She felt he would work as quickly as possible and that they'd hear about the "low hanging fruit" that he could uncover relatively soon.

They all discussed that this step meant that "we're in this through the end," and hopefully, it would result in the restoration of Harvey's estate. Tory interjected the warning that Ted had given and that whoever was responsible would do anything to avoid getting caught. The impressive overall tenor of the conversation was that all three were fearless and convinced that they were doing what was right and necessary.

Next, Walt spoke up. "I have a present for each of you." He brought three bags from under the table, kept one of them, and handed one to Harv and Tory. He said, "These are the

Tracfones sometimes known as "burn phones" for each of us. I took the Wildstone bus to the mall and went into Walmart. I'm pretty sure that nobody that we know saw me purchase the phones. There were only a couple of people on the bus, and they went to the movies. As I thought about this," Walt went on, "I figured we should do our normal business from our Wildstone phones, so there's no suspicion as if we were to stop using them altogether. We should use our cell phones for our confidential calls, texts, emails, etc. You can even do Google searches on these. They are not quite iPhones, but they work well. I've had your phone numbers written on the piece of paper in the box. Let's take them out, power them up, and spend a little time learning how to use them. Then we'll load them with one another's phone number. Also, put in your phone number in case you don't remember it. Later on, you can put other numbers in them also." Tory interjected, "We each need to enter Ted Hame's number as well, and I'll give him all of your numbers." Then Walt said, "By the way, you each owe me $90.00. That's for the Samsung Galaxy phone and tax. I chose these because they will do pretty much what we want them to do, you know, pictures, texts, email, and internet searches for a good price. The guy said these are good phones. Whenever we get low on minutes, we can go and buy more time. I've loaded them with 6 hours. Let's see how long that will last us. We can reload them online, so we don't have to go to the store. Harv, be careful not to use the computer in the main building library. If they're checking on you, you don't want them to be able to see your searches." Harvey agreed. "Can I use your computer here?" Walt affirmed that, and Tory said that they could switch around to be safe.

They powered them up, and as they talked and drank, they entered the numbers, figured out the phones, and they all felt better. Harv struggled a bit because he had always had iPhones, and the android system worked differently.

Again, their meals were delivered to Walt's apartment. Harv wondered out loud if sending his and Tory's meals to Walt's place might arouse suspicion if they were being observed. Maybe so, the others agreed, except that most of the independent living people at Wildstone had friends with whom they would spend most of their time rather than be alone. It was something to think about. If Harvey was being watched, they all agreed they didn't want to make themselves targets also. Tory said, "Why don't we change the places we eat? And, if I eat here, I still can get my food delivered to my apartment and then bring it down the hallway to Walt's, or you can come to my place." "Great idea," said Harvey. "Let's plan on mixing it up a bit." As they ate, and afterward, they spoke about the next steps in their plan.

First, they thanked Walt for procuring their phones and Tory for her call with Ted Hame. They all expressed lots of interest in finding out more from him. Next, Harvey filled them in. "Folks, I'm more than a bit concerned. I had Brenda Williams, my Charge Nurse, buy me some clothes, as you know. I hung them up and put them away. Last night, when I got ready for bed, I could have sworn they were not hung where and in the order that I had hung them. I don't know who would go through my things. I believe Brenda is trustworthy." Walt said, "Yeah, and she knew what she had purchased for you so she wouldn't have to go through them."

Harvey went on. "I asked Brenda if she could look at the log and find out who came into my corridor and might have signed in per policy. I think somebody went through my stuff. With that in mind, I asked Brenda to tell Charlene, Culpepper's secretary, that I had my house keys and was going to take a cab over the next few days to check on my house and belongings. I still have the house key, but I asked her to find an old key, and we'll tag it as England House and put it in my nightstand drawer to see if it's taken. I think Culpepper if he's involved, will take the bait and try to do something to keep me from going to my house."

"That's brilliant," said Tory. "But I'm afraid that you're going to force his hand such that he'll have to do something, and I'm not sure that it will be good for you." Walt came up with the same caution saying, "Harv, be careful not to take any of the medicine that they give you, especially if it's a new prescription. One way to control patients and even make them seem mentally incompetent is through drugs. It would even keep others from taking you seriously and from investigating any of your claims."

Now all three of them were a bit anxious. They had no idea of the depths to which the hoax went and no idea of the tools that Wildstone or Culpepper could use. They asked the question.

"So, what can, or could they possibly do?" Tory asked. "Let's brainstorm. Maybe they have tools, but so do we." Walt said, "You know the intercoms in each room and apartment used for emergencies or to call the desk or nurses' stations? Could those somehow be used to listen in to our places? If so, how would we know?" Harvey interjected, "I'm also bothered by the fact that so many people have keys to our places, and we are not allowed to have locks changed supposedly so we can get service in case of a medical emergency. Is there any way to prevent it or at least know if people are coming in?" "What about cameras?" Tory asked. "We know there are cameras throughout the grounds and hallways. What about our rooms. Is there any chance we either have cameras on us already or could have if they become suspicious?"

As they discussed the situation, they agreed to tape covers or small pillows over the intercoms whenever they met. Harv suggested that they use small pieces of transparent tape in unsuspected locations so they would know if people had entered their places or even opened drawers when they were gone. Maybe even they should have their discussions outside. They were all most concerned about Harvey. He was the one who had the problem. They all agreed, including Harv, that the reasons were that he was not expected to live, and he had considerable assets that either Culpepper or Wildstone or both wanted to grab. Not suspecting that he would survive, much less thrive, they had acted to confiscate his money and property. Harvey was still worried that his house and other assets would somehow be taken as well. But he thought he had to have his confirmation of identity (birth certificate and passport) from his safety deposit box and then go to the County Clerks' office to check out his deed. Hopefully, his comment to Brenda would get some reaction that would tip Culpepper's hand. They agreed to meet the following afternoon in the courtyard at 4:00 p.m. to discuss the next steps. They all agreed. Harvey and Walt also decided to meet at 9:00 in the morning at the PT room for more conditioning.

When Harvey returned to his room just after 8:00 p.m., he found a note on his desk from Brenda with her phone number asking him to call her at home. He took out his new phone, entered her number into the contacts, walked out the double doors to the courtyard, and called her. She answered, "Brenda Williams." Harvey identified himself and told her he thought this was a secure call because of his new cell phone. Brenda sighed. "Harvey, I'm worried. I searched the visitor's log, and an unusual name was signed in. Charles Bilford of Wildstone's law firm and Anthony Culpepper's best buddy was in your corridor last night. He would also have access to a passkey because he's on the Board of Directors. What would he want with your room?"

"If he's involved," Harvey said, "It could make sense. He wants to know what my suspicions are and what I know.

Thank goodness my notes, wallet, bank card, etc. were either with me or in my locked compartment. But that won't stop them for long." Brenda also said that she had mentioned in passing to Charlene that you would be going home to check on your home and furnishings later in the week. "I'm apprehensive about your situation, Harv. If he's involved, he will have to do something to end this. He or someone who works for him will have to stop you." Brenda said, "Wait for me, Harvey. I'll be there in about 15 minutes. I live very close." Harvey agreed. Brenda arrived and met him in the courtyard.

Harvey said, "Yeah, Brenda, I've thought about it. Probably the best thing you can do is review my medicine to ensure they don't try to load me up on something that will make me muddy or mentally incompetent or to seem that way; maybe even do me significant harm." Brenda said that she would review his meds to ensure the only meds he would get are his blood pressure medicine. She also told Harvey not to accept any meds from someone other than her." Harvey thanked her profusely. Brenda was an essential and important person to him. Brenda asked Harv, "Why did you want to talk outside?" He responded, "I guess I'm a bit paranoid that others could be listening in.

In fact, let me ask you if the intercom in my room can be turned on from some other place to listen to activity in my room?" Brenda thought about it and replied, "Absolutely, yes! I hadn't thought of that. We can turn the intercoms on so we can hear the patient if they are in distress and any cries for help." "Brenda, could the intercoms be listened to by only Mr. Culpepper?" Brenda replied, "I don't know, but I imagine they could. He could let himself into the control room, punch a few buttons, and listen to whomever he wanted." Harvey was now convinced that he, Tory, and Walt had better be careful. "Is there any way we could know if we were being listened to, Brenda?" Brenda thought deeply and finally answered, "Harv, do you know the red button that you push to talk to the nurses' station? We'll try this when we go back to your room. If you press and hold the red button, before you say anything, you can hear the background noise from the nurses' station. If you were to press the red button expecting to talk to the nurse, and you heard zero background noise, it would be because they are listening to you." Harvey thought about it and asked, "Is there any way for them to listen to us outside?" Brenda said that she didn't know it could be done.

"Let's go back to the room together," said Harv. Upon returning to the room, Brenda closed his door, went to the wall intercom, and pressed the red button expecting to hear noise from the nurses' station. There was nothing; no noise. Brenda made the "Shhhhhh" sign by putting her index finger up to her lips. She left the room, beckoning Harv to follow. They walked down the hall to an empty room and went in. Brenda pressed the red button and held it down, and they immediately heard the computer and printer noises and monitors from the nurses' station. Brenda said, "They're listening to you. Don't say anything or use the phone for anything important." Harv said, "Who is listening to me?" Brenda shrugged her shoulders, but they both knew it was Culpepper or his friend Bilford. Brenda went down to the nurses' station to confirm that there was no listening going on from there.

Wildstone violated both of their trust. Harv felt good that he had a lockable locker in the room but still didn't feel comfortable leaving anything important there.

The Bad Guys' First Step

At 9:00 a.m. the next morning, both Harvey and Walt were right on time at the PT workout room. They were both feeling good and looking forward to a good session. As before, they started with some good stretching. It was surprising how much better it felt than their first session. They then did several reps of push-ups and leg lifts. It would have been evident to any observer that their balance, coordination, and strength were returning. And of course, the trash talk continued among the friends. Before they left, both of them practiced some of their old defensive moves from their close order combat training. They both thought, "Some things you just don't forget."

They agreed that again they would meet at 3:00 p.m. but this time at Tory's apartment, 5G. Walt said to look at her patio to see if they were out there before going into the building. Harv also whispered to Walt that he wanted to speak to him as they left the building. Walt caught on, and they turned to stroll out of the room. As they approached the door, a man dressed in white approached Harvey with a syringe in hand. He said to Harvey, "John ordered a B12 shot for you. It will help you get back your strength faster." Harv looked at the man and asked his name. "Adam," he replied. Harv said, "Well, Adam, John's a good P.T. but cannot order prescriptions. Before I take it, please show the prescription to me." Adam looked surprised but came at Harv's left arm with the syringe anyway. That was a mistake. Harv quickly raised his left arm in a deflective whack and knocked the syringe out of his hand, and when Adam tried to swing back, Harv's right fist caught him hard just below the forehead. Adam tried to rebound, but Walt put him in a half-nelson from the back. These two old guys defeated Adam. He looked dejected.

"Who sent you?" growled Harv. When Adam snickered, Walt snapped Adam's head forward toward his chest. "Ow," Adam said. "I don't know. I work in memory care and got a note from the big boss telling me I needed to make sure I gave you this shot even if you didn't want it!" "Who is your big boss?" asked Harv while he looked ready to punch young Adam's light out. "It's Chris Blanner." Walt asked while putting more pressure on Adam, "Who does he report to?"

"Mr. Culpepper. He reports to Anthony Culpepper."

As they prepared to let him go, they told Adam not to underestimate the older men, especially the veterans, and he'd

109

better tell no one of their interaction. Adam went to retrieve the syringe. As he put his hand down to get it off of the floor, Harv's foot went down hard on his hand. Harv said, "That belongs to me now, punk. Go away fast!"

Walt and Harvey sat on the bench press benches, physically and mentally worn out. Finally, Walt said, "Harv, we're in for it now. He will report it, and they will try to get us for acting violent or crazy or both. Or fine us for assault. I wonder what they were going to give you." "That's why I wanted the syringe," said Harv. "After Brenda and I spoke last night, and I'll tell you more later, I think it was a drug that would make me comatose, or mess up my thinking... something that would make me easier to deal with. We're going to have to meet earlier. I have a lot to tell you." They both agreed that they would shower, get their notebooks and phones, and meet for lunch at Tory's. "I'll call her and work it out," said Walt. As they left, Harvey picked up the syringe and handed it to Walt. "If this is important, they will look for it in my room. We need to get this to Tory to have her friend evaluate it." "Roger that," Walt said.

They returned to their respective areas to clean up before meeting for lunch at Tory's. Things were getting profoundly serious now. Something would happen fast, Harv thought. And he also thought they would get dangerous.

Harvey reached his room, locked the doors behind himself, and pressed the red intercom button. He heard nothing, so he knew someone was listening. He took a slow shower and thought about things. If this got progressively more serious, the penalties for Anthony Culpepper, the lawyer Bilford and maybe even Wildstone would be very harsh. They would likely do anything to try to save themselves. Harvey turned off the water, dried, and put on his robe. He heard some shuffling in the room. He ran in to find a young nurse looking through the desk and nightstand. He grabbed her hands and asked, "What the hell are you doing in my room?" She was frightened and told Harvey that she was told to go into Harvey's room and find a syringe left in there by mistake and retrieve it to the nurses' station to keep Harv from hurting himself. Someone would come by later to pick it up.

Harvey told her, "There is no syringe here, period. Take a look." He opened his dresser drawers, his closet, his nightstand, and even his locked locker. She satisfied herself. Harvey then asked the young woman, "I'm of very sound mind and body. What would you do if you found someone in your house or apartment looking through your things?" She said she'd call the police. Harvey then told her maybe I should call them. The nurse told Harv that the nursing home had the right to enter any domicile on its property to offer care. Harvey told her firmly that her trip had nothing to do with providing care. He then asked, "Who was going to come to pick up the syringe?" She said that Mr. Culpepper himself said he had to be in this corridor, so he'd go ahead and pick it up. Harv asked, "What's your name?" She replied, "Linda Pegwell, and I'm not a thief!" Harvey told her that she'd do well never, ever to enter his room again without advanced notice and his permission. As she left, she was shaken but calm.

Harvey quickly dressed, took his notebook, wallet and phone, and headed out to meet Tory and Walt. He stopped at the nurses' station and didn't see Linda. He asked the other nurse where Linda was. "Linda just took a break," Harv said thanks, and as he walked, he knew she was calling Culpepper's office.

Harvey noticed that both Walt and Tory were on her patio. They were a bit early, thank goodness. As Harvey sat down, his great agitation showed. Both asked him what was wrong. Harvey related the happening to them, and Walt had already filled Tory in about the scuffle with Adam earlier. Harvey said, "It's happening full blast now. They will be working overtime to get me out of the picture. I'm not sure they know anyone else is involved. They probably think Walt was just protecting me this morning." Tory said, "Walt and I agree. There is no stopping it now. Walt has the syringe, and I've emailed Ted to see if we can have it tested. We need to know how far they will go. I'm hoping he has a contact locally who can test the substance, tell us about it and send an official report to Ted. We can't let them stop us!"

They talked about Harv's discussion with Brenda and how the intercoms can be used to listen to the patients. As Harv talked about Linda Pegwell, the nurse who was searching through his room while he was there, they concluded that the young nurse was told that Harvey would harm himself, so she had to act boldly. It was a good thing the syringe was not in Harvey's room because if it had been retrieved, Anthony Culpepper would be able to deny everything. Tory had made some tasty BLT's with some chips and iced tea, so they ate and felt much better. Then they went to Tory's intercom and pressed the red button and held it for a moment. They heard the noises from the corridor and the "concierge." At least for now, she was off the hook. Then they went next door to Walt's apartment and again pressed the red button, holding it down. They heard absolutely nothing. Using his finger to his lips, he warned them not to say anything while they returned next door to Tory's.

"They're onto us," said Walt to Harvey. They thought it might have just been since this morning's event. Nonetheless, they realized they were being surveilled. Tory's place would be next, but at least they knew how to detect if they were being listened to. About that time, Tory checked her email. She said that Ted Hame was actually on his way from Chicago. She relayed that he had just finished up a story, rented a car, and drove down. He figured he'd be there for dinner. They were all excited and anxious.

Their concern was that it had gone far enough. Culpepper had to stop Harvey England or be stopped himself! This situation could be very dangerous at the least for Harvey.

Deep in the Conflict

Charles Bilford and Anthony Culpepper spoke in dubious and low tones. They were both frightened about what might happen... to themselves, Wildstone Senior Living Community, and their fortunes.

Bilford said, "To put it straight, Mr. Harvey England cannot be allowed to continue. I heard you say that you have information that he will check on his house and belongings. He cannot be allowed to do so. When he finds out that it's been sold to new owners, he will call the police. He might have already done so."

Anthony Culpepper replied, "I don't think so. I've been monitoring his phone use from his room, and there are no such calls. I think he's suspicious, but as long as he's been here, there's no evidence that he knows we've siphoned his assets. We just can't let him get to that point." Charles said, "How do we prevent that? He'll either have to become a bumbling vegetable or die!"

Both of them thought for a moment, and Anthony spoke up. "This morning I sent one of our staff, Adam, to give

England a 'B-12' shot. That would have solved the problem. But England and Schell fought back and prevented Adam from giving the shot. But we'll keep trying. The trick will be not to be so apparent that it arouses any suspicion at all."

"So, have we learned anything from listening to his activities in his room? I know I didn't learn anything. I think I heard him talking to someone at his bank, but I'm not sure. I thought we had everything covered, but obviously not." Bilson said.

"What about Mr. Schell. Is he involved in helping England?" Bilson continued. Anthony replied, "To believe that would be to believe that they are a couple of competent detectives who are working to put us away. No way. They are a couple of old men, pretty sharp maybe, but old men spending time together. Besides, we've also been listening to Schell, and there's nothing there. They have dinner at night and enjoy one another's company." Charles Bilford asked, "How long have you listened to them?" "Just started last night," said Culpepper. "Let's hope you're right," replied Charles. "If we get caught, we lose everything!"

Charlene chimed on the intercom. Culpepper asked why she interrupted his meeting, and she said it was an important call from Linda Pegwell. Culpepper took it and put it on his speaker. "Mr. Culpepper, I did what you said. I didn't know that Mr. England was in his room and he came out of the shower and caught me. He was furious!"

"So, what did you do or tell him?" Culpepper asked. She said, "I explained that some important medication might have been left in his room, and I was trying to find it. He settled down and let me go through everything in his room, and the syringe wasn't there. I think he was angrier that I came into his room without permission. When I left, he was just fine." Mr. Culpepper told her, "That's OK, Linda. Thanks for letting me know." He hung up.

"You see, Charles; England doesn't have a clue, and thank goodness he doesn't have the syringe. Without a sample of the contents, he can't prove a thing. And he has no idea how to know what's in the syringe. Even if he's angry, he can't do anything! We are in control. We provide everything for him! He is completely reliant upon us, even if he doesn't think so. We're smarter than he is and his friends! They are just old, feeble-minded people."

Charles agreed. Tony went on, "They can't stand up to us. We're in charge, Charles. We own them!"

J. Carl Goodman

We Now Have Enough!

Tory, Walt, and Harvey were still talking around Tory's patio table as they waited to meet the famed Ted Hame.

All of a sudden, Walt became very animated. "If we have an hour to wait, I'm going to go check on the deed to Harv's house. I've been bugged about this. I have the address, and I believe the tax records and deeds are of public record. I'll bet I can find out." He took out his cell phone and googled the courthouse and punched some buttons. He stepped off to the side as not to interfere with Harv and Tory's discussion. Tory made a lot of sense, even though she seemed a bit paranoid to Harvey! She said, "They may have their suspicions about us, but I don't think they believe that we know as much as we do. They think we are bumbling old people who get in their way. They still don't want to get caught, so you continue to be in danger." They both agreed and continued their talk. "Harv," Tory said, "you must be most careful."

Just as Mr. Culpepper and Bilford had come to that conclusion, Harvey and Tory arrived at the same. They discussed the fact that everything from their toilets to rooms was under Wildstone's control. Harvey said, "Let's go through a sample day. We get up, get ready for the day, get dressed, and Walt and I work out. Then we go back to our places, get cleaned up, eat breakfast, and then read, watch TV, or visit one another. Then comes lunch, the rest of the day, and then dinner. If they want to get to us, what's the obvious method?" Tory listened and had a sudden revelation. "It's the food, Harv. It's the food!"

Harv asked, "The food?" Tory responded. "I listened to your little overview and made some connections. You did leave out that we're given our medications, but we know what they look like, and it would be tough to substitute meds without involving the nurses. You trust Brenda, don't you?" "Without question," Harvey replied. "Well then," Tory continued, "Wildstone is involved in everything we do while we're here. What is the easiest way they could harm you or even all of us, for that matter? The food! Every day they have three chances and many different side dishes to tamper with. Some substances could harm you; even kill you that are very hard to detect in food. Plus, those who work in the kitchen could easily be directed to give you or any of us a specific plate without suspicion, especially if the order came from on high. Yes, I believe the most dangerous thing will be the food."

By that time, Walt had learned what he needed and was listening to this ongoing conversation. It made such sense. He chimed in, "I agree with Tory, Harv. They need to kill or disable you, and maybe they think me too at this point. The food is the best way. They could doctor up dishes until you ate one, or they could put small amounts of a substance in dishes over a short period so you would appear to get sicker and sicker. We'd never know it. We need to mention this to Ted Hame when he gets here!"

From the courtyard came a voice, "Did somebody call me?" Ted laughed, came up to the table, and gave Tory a big hug and a smooch on the cheek. Tory introduced Ted to Harv and Walt. Ted sat down. Walt interrupted before anything was said. "Harv, our suspicions sadly were correct. Somehow your house was sold, and there are new owners on the deed. I'm sorry, buddy." Ted said, "That's awful. I've heard of these scams, but this is the first one I'll be involved with. I will certainly help. Has anyone checked on your Social Security and pension payments yet?" The answer was no, but Ted could help with that.

The next hour was spent catching Ted up on all of the nefarious things that had happened and on the evidence they had gathered and even the hunches they had. They went to Walt's apartment and showed him the difference in the intercom systems between his and Tory's. They told him about their new cell phones and made sure they exchanged numbers. They then presented the syringe, still with the needle guard attached, to Ted, asking if he could get the substance evaluated. He happened to know someone in the lab at Christie Clinic and would get them working on it first thing in the morning. He went out right away and hid it in his rental car.

Harv, who had been a bit distracted based on the bad news he had heard from Walt, was back in the conversation with full attention now. He had an idea. If Ted could pose as Tory's beloved nephew who would be visiting for a while, they could go into Walt's apartment and talk about it where the intercom could pick it up. Because Walt's place had a small second bedroom, Ted could stay there and, it would give them perfect excuses to order food for delivery. Ted asked about their fear of the food, and they filled him in regarding their conclusion that it would be particularly dangerous for Harv, and the food was the most obvious way to neutralize him.

Ted agreed with them but asked that they give him a pseudonym because if they checked him out with his real name, it would be a giveaway. They decided his name would be Ted Randall. By using the same family name as Tory, it would not be unusual. Ted also suggested that Harvey, under the ruse of saving money, would order his regular meal and have it delivered to Walt's place. They would still order out, but Ted would keep Harv's plate from Wildstone and have it tested for substances. Ted also warned them about maintaining a chain of evidence that was not tainted nor touched by others. They would also make a note of when and who delivered the food from Wildstone. They all agreed that if they were right, answers would come quickly. Ted also recommended that Harvey get his important papers, cards, and money out of his room. Because they would eat at Walt's, and Harv would have his Wildstone meal delivered to Walt's place, Harvey decided to go back to his room to get his things.

Harv thought a lot about the things that they had discussed. The loss of his home was devastating. He tried to keep a stiff upper lip, but it was hard. Although Harv was one who did not care so much about stuff, it was hard to realize that the art, décor, and Tiffany lamps of Margaret's might be gone forever! He was also worried about his precious

Mustang. Harv, like many men, didn't deal with emotions well. He was tired of this. He had lost much of everything only because he had become ill, and some lowlife, swindling, cheating thief illegally took it from him at his worst point. Harv became angry. He swore he would get Anthony Culpepper, and he would not make it painless for him!

As he walked down the corridor to his room, the door was ajar. He noticed it as he approached. He opened the door slowly and saw nobody there, but before he entered, he went to the nurses' station and asked the duty nurse, Glenda, if she had been in his room. She replied to the negative. Harvey asked her who else could have been in there. She, without concern, answered that any of the many who had keys could have been there; maintenance, safety, security, food service, and any of the managers. Harvey needed to hide a camera!

He then went into his room. He noticed that somebody had been searching and didn't even try to hide it. His drawers were opened, and his clothes were askew. His perfectly made bed, a long-held habit from the military, had the sheet pulled out, and the mattress was crooked. His few books and magazines were sitting on his side chair. The drawer in his nightstand was open, and the fake house key he had planted was no longer there. He had marked it with a dot of a green marker, so it would be easy to spot!

Harvey went over to his small, locked cabinet and noticed someone had started to remove the hinges to give them access to his things. He may have come back and almost caught them in the act because a kitchen knife they had used as a screwdriver was lying on the desk with a bent tip, and the lower hinge was half removed. Harvey closed the door, unlocked this cabinet, and pulled out his personal paperwork and important other personal items. He then reattached the hinge, relocked the cupboard, and went to the nurses' station. He was pissed!

He approached the duty nurse, Glenda, and said, "Come with me, now!" with such authority she followed. He opened his door and showed her the mess. He acted furiously, even though he had expected such an intrusion. Harvey told her, "I'll be watching. If I catch anyone in my room, I will kick some ass! Do you understand? This is my temporary home, and I will defend it. You tell them all. I will call the police and have this investigated, and I will call the News Gazette and have them publicize it. We'll see how Wildstone gets away with that!" The duty nurse was in tears. "How could you have let that happen?" asked Harvey. She said, "The only person I saw near your room was Mr. Culpepper. He wouldn't have done anything like that. He's the boss!"

Now Harvey knew for sure!

Harvey said, "For the next day or few, I'll be eating my meals at Walt Schell's place to spend some time with Ted Randall. Please make sure my meals are sent to Walt's apartment." He received confirmation. He then told her to file a complaint with management about the apparent "break-in" to his room. Harv told her he would expect a copy of it to be waiting at the nurses' station when he returned. He also told her he would let the media know about this! Once Glenda left, Harvey took out his cell phone and took some pictures. He wanted something to show anyone who took an interest!

It is Escalated!

After putting things away in their proper place and checking for anything missing other than the planted house key, Harv, with his important papers, wallet, and money in tow, headed to Walt's. He was anxious to tell the others what had happened. He was just glad that Culpepper didn't get to his wallet with his bank card, money, pictures of Margaret, and other important information or notes and contacts.

When he arrived at Walt's, nobody was outside, and nobody answered his door. He was worried but went next door to Tory's, and she responded to the doorbell. As soon as Harv entered, he pressed the red intercom button and heard nothing. He knew they were being monitored at Tory's now. He whispered to the others, and they responded that they had checked when they came in, noticed they were being watched, and just talked like friends and relatives to maintain Ted's cover. Harv then walked into Tory's living room, took a small lumbar pillow from a chair, and asked for some tape. Tory provided the tape, and Harv fastened the pillow over the intercom. "That should stop them," he said.

They sat down in her small but beautifully decorated living room, and Harvey related what had happened in his room. Ted told him that the most disturbing thing is that Culpepper had neither tried to hide his appearance nor carefully try to cover the search of Harvey's room. Harv pulled out his phone and produced the pictures for them to see. Walt agreed and stated, "I think this likely means that Culpepper knows that you know; may suspect that we also know, and is now in the mode to destroy any evidence you have against him. That also means he will try to destroy you, so you can't raise the issue of what he did to you with forged documents!" Harv chimed in and said, "I've raised the alarm because I told Glenda to fill out a major complaint that would get sent to the Board of Directors, and I expected to receive a copy when I returned tonight. I also told her I would like to send it to the press."

Tory expressed that Harvey's threat would escalate this, and Anthony Culpepper and Charles Bilford would feel like they had no choice but to stop Harv immediately. She said, "This is alarming. They will have to orchestrate something to shut you up! They could use medication, taint your food, or even risk a scandal like claiming another patient murdered you because of delusions or whatever. But there's no time left.

They will feel that they must take action. They may even act against us if they feel that we may become a threat, especially if something happens to you! Harvey, have you spoken with your friend Brenda recently?" Harv responded, saying, "Tory, you just raised another issue. I haven't seen Brenda in the last two days. I'm just hoping that she is just taking a couple of days off."

Listening to this exchange began to eat at Ted. He was getting anxious about both Tory and his new friends. As they had spoken, Ted realized that they were correct. If Anthony Culpepper and his confidant Charles Bilford had forged documents to strip Harv of his money and property, neither could afford to have their actions come to light. By now, they will have realized that they were not dealing with feeble old people who were plagued by mental weakness and fear. These were competent victims of the crime and would take the two to the task. All because Harv didn't die after all!

Ted suggested that they all go out to the small patio and gather at the table. As they sat down, Ted said, "I've investigated lots of bad stuff, but this is looking as dangerous as it gets. I agree with Tory, Harv. I believe you're in great danger. Tory and Walt maybe also, but I hope we've successfully avoided saying anything that raises their suspicions. I have to go to my car for something; I'll be right back."

Harv looked a bit despondent. Walt asked, "What wrong, buddy?" Harv looked at both Tory and Walt and said he felt so badly that he might have gotten them involved in this dangerous activity without realizing just how bad the situation could be. Both of them told Harv that it was the most satisfying and exciting thing they had done in years. Tory said, "We should be able to do this for others too!"

Ted returned from the rental car and handed Harv a heavy metal device. "This is a door lock," said Ted. "As you can see, you put it at the bottom of the door jam and step on the button. It expands, and the door will not open from the outside. Use it when you go back to your room tonight. Even somebody with a passkey will not get in. I use it when I'm on assignments and staying in hotels feeling insecure. It works well." Harv took it, looked it over, and put it in his pocket. Tory said, "We should order dinner soon." Everyone agreed, and Harv interjected that he had told Glenda to send his dinner to Walt's place. When the others looked confused, Harv said, "When Ted said he would have the syringe contents analyzed, I decided if the food were the obvious way to get to us, I would order my meal as regular and give it to Ted to have it analyzed too." "Great idea, Harv," said Ted. Tory went online to look at the menu from Papa Del's pizza for delivery. "It's been the best in the region for years and years," she said. They selected two medium pizzas: one with their thick Sicilian crust and one with the thin American crust. "They'll be here in about 45 minutes," she said. They poured some red wine and had some cheese and crackers while they waited.

Their timing was good. About 20 minutes later, Harvey's meal was delivered to Walt's. "You the only one eating tonight?" asked the orderly? "No," said Walt. "I just didn't want to spend the money ordering in." The orderly said, "You're cheap like me," and chucked. "Have a good evening," he said as he left.

Ted grabbed the meal. Through the lid, it looked good as most of the Wildstone meals were. It was Chicken Parmesan, mixed veggies, and a nice sized Caesar Salad. He put it in the fridge until he went to Christie Clinic in the morning. Shortly after that, the pizza was delivered. Ted insisted on paying. He told them he could see a big story coming from this adventure. They sat down and truly enjoyed the pizza. It was excellent, a real break from their regular fare, and they were confident it wouldn't kill them!

After they ate, Harv asked Ted what he thought about the situation. Ted responded, "You know, Harv, when I first heard about this, I thought it was likely a few old folks whose minds or fears had taken over. I had heard, as we all have, of homes taking advantage of seniors' assets, but I thought what I initially heard was over the top. But then, as I saw what has happened to you, learned about the monitoring through the intercoms, your missing investments and now home, the 'assault' with the syringe, and then your room being trashed, I'm convinced this is a big issue. Tomorrow, we'll know more after the food and the syringe are evaluated."

Harvey then said, "I'm thinking of creating a real rat's nest. I will tell Brenda that I want to see the bill and the effect of my Medicare, social security, and pension payments applied to the bill so far. I also want to change the delivery of my social security and pension to my checking account. I'll also directly ask what happened to my assets. What do you think?"

Walt agreed. "It has to be done. They know that you know by now." Tory interjected, "I agree, Walt, but I'm not so sure that Harv is the one who should be asking the question. They are already targeting him and even us because we're looking into this mess. Maybe someone else should be asking."

Ted intervened. "As I listen to you, folks, I tend to agree with Tory. The more they think this 'look-see' is being done by you folks in their home, the more they will believe that they can stop it, and they'll keep trying. But if someone outside this asks them about all of this, it will become more prominent than them. Perhaps someone in the Illinois Dep't of Public Health. I'll look into it. In the meantime, we must ensure that we compile and document the calls Harv had with the broker about his investments, the banker about his accounts, and then verify Walt's conversations about Harv's property. We need a proper investigation by someone who is licensed and authorized to conduct such a study. You can bet that Culpepper and Charles Bilford will be scared to death of it. And, once Wildstone corporate offices hear about it, they will be gunning for both of them also. We will have to be careful."

The Proof of Harm

Harvey returned to his room that evening with a wide range of thoughts and emotions. He was so angry; he wondered how he could ever get his life back or his home, personal property, and money. Harv was worried about putting his friends in possible danger, yet completely committed to following this path until the most logical conclusion; that Anthony Culpepper and Charles Bilford, at minimum, were put in prison for a long time.

His room looked fine when he returned. There was a cupcake with a note from Jason stating that he was sorry he had missed Harv and saved him a cupcake. Harv didn't touch it but smiled a bit to see Jason's note. Harv then pressed the red intercom button to hear nothing at all, so he confirmed it was not safe to talk openly within his room. Harv thought about a proper investigation by the appropriate authorities and knew that Ted would know how to get them involved. With thoughts of Brenda, Harv left his room, locked the door, and headed out to the courtyard. Once he was sure he was not detected or followed, he pulled out his phone and called Brenda's home number. He was relieved when she answered.

"Brenda," he said, "I've missed seeing you, and with all that's going on, I wanted to see if you're OK." Brenda sighed and responded, "Thanks, Harvey. It's good to know I'm missed. I received a call from Charlene saying that my schedule had changed and that I should take a long weekend and then a day's vacation before returning. I thought it was odd, but because I am a nursing manager, it was not unusual for me to hear from Charlene. Is everything OK?" Harv replied that it was but that things were going to start happening quickly. Brenda assured that she would come to see Harvey as soon as she returned to work and then implored him to be very careful. She even told him to make sure that when he and Walt went to work out that they wipe down all the equipment both for COVID and anything else. Harv got her point and said they would. After they talked, Harv sat down on a bench and just thought for a while.

When he returned to his room, he locked his door and then placed the door jamb lock that Ted had provided. Harv then sat in his chair and, in his notebook, recorded everything that had happened, who was involved, what they said, and made sure the order of the happenings was correct. He included everything from the time he began to emerge from his fog, making a note of who he met and his impressions of them. He even made sure that his first interaction with Anthony Culpepper was described. He included how he met Walt, Tory, and now Ted and some of their excellent sleuthing together. He recorded the tussle with Adam, finding Linda Pegwell in his room, and all the other things. Harv prepared himself for bed.

He rested well until about 2:15 a.m., according to his nightstand clock. He seemed to hear a scraping noise that woke him. He sat up and realized someone had unlocked his door and was trying to get in. The lock that Ted had provided met the challenge and prevented whoever was trying to get in from doing so, especially without calling attention to the fact. Harvey flew from his bed to the door, hit the release button on the extra lock, and opened the door. He saw no one but, of course, wondered who it was and why someone, in fact, anyone, would attempt to enter his room while he was asleep. He could only come to one conclusion ...they knew he was there and maybe trying to sneak in and give him a substance to hurt, maim, or kill him! This was just getting way too ugly. Harv reset the extra door lock, locked his deadbolt, and went back to bed. He did not sleep well until he faded away around 4:30 a.m.

As a matter of habit, he awoke before 7:30 a.m., even as tired as he was. He took his time as he got up and brushed his teeth. He dressed in workout clothes as he would meet Walt at 9:00 or maybe a little before. He went out to the nurses' station and asked the nurse if she had seen anyone around his room a little after 2:00 a.m. She calmly responded that she had taken her break precisely at that time and went to the cafeteria to eat her 2:15 a.m. lunch and relax. Harvey quickly came to the conclusion that whoever tried to get into his room, knew her schedule. He went back to his room and recorded the information in his notebook. Today, when he walked to the exercise room to meet Walt, he took his spiral notebook, phone and wallet with him along with his special door lock. He did not want to lose his notebook or wallet and felt a good chance of that happening if he left them in his room.

Walt, true to form, was waiting for Harv when he arrived. They greeted each other with a high five and a big smile. Each knew that without the other, it would be a much more tedious and inconsequential life. They went into the room, and Harv mentioned that Brenda had told him that both of them should clean the equipment before they touched it as a precaution. It made sense, so they both got to the task using the wipes that were regularly provided. Walt went to the intercom and, as they did in their rooms, pressed the red call button, and listened. They could hear the sounds of the office and realized nobody was listening to them at that moment. As they did their stretches, Harv told Walt about last night. They were both alarmed but not surprised. Walt said, "Isn't it ridiculous that we expect this type of thing to happen here?" They both agreed. Then the funniest thing happened.

Both men had been working on their core strength, their arm strength, leg strength, speed, balance, coordination, and aerobic stamina. Walt, on a trip to the Wildstone library, found an old VHS of Billy Banks "Tai Bo" videos and put them in the old machine in the workout room. Harv looked disgusted, but as Walt started working with the footage, Harv joined in. Both were huffing and puffing but pressing on as they did punches and kicks to the music. It was comical but sure gave them a workout and some new punches! They finished, left the room, and headed to their places to clean up and meet for lunch together. They both wondered if Ted had managed to find his laboratory friend to analyze the contents of the syringe and Harv's dinner from last night. They, of course, had their suspicions, but the proof would be helpful and necessary.

They split up to go their ways, and Harvey returned to his room. While both were concerned, Harv took a long shower, shaved, and cleaned up well with no negative issues. He had a few minutes, so he went to the lobby and read the paper before going to meet Walt, Tory, and Ted for lunch and essential discussion. Harvey had made some notes to make sure they covered the most critical issues.

Harv took a stroll over to Walt's place and carried his notebook with him. He also carried his "extra" door lock because he didn't expect it to be in his room if he left it there. He now also took his phone and wallet wherever went. It was sad, he thought, that there was no trust left in this place. In reality, it was worse than that. There was no trust plus the fear that harm could come to one or all of their friends! He pondered the chances that others over the years had similar instances of theft or manipulation of their finances or property; or even worse, physical injury or death!

He heard them talking as he walked to their courtyard. The trees and bushes muffled most of the conversation, so Harvey couldn't understand them until he was very close. As they saw him approach, each offered the other's greetings. Walt told Harv to "take a load off" and offered him a glass of lemonade. Tory had made some chicken salad sandwiches and macaroni salad for lunch. It looked good! Tory admonished them that they would wait for Ted's return before they ate. Both Walt and Harv made like they were pouting, and Tory laughed out loud. After they jokingly called her mean and tough, they began to talk. Harv hesitated to tell his whole story knowing it would have to be repeated once Ted returned. He did tell them about his conversation with Brenda. They all concluded that Culpepper, Bilford and maybe even Charlene, if she was involved, knew that Brenda was supportive of Harv and wanted her out of the way for a few days. Were they expecting to do Harvey or his friends some harm while she was off duty? Who knew? All of them had speculated so much that they were ready for some evidence and proof of their suspicions!

Ted returned from his errands, and, after ringing Walt's doorbell to no avail, walked around the building and joined them outside. Walt chided Ted about the fact that they all had to wait for his return to eat. As they dug into the food Tory had provided, Ted said, "I spoke with my friend. He has the syringe and food. He said he would run some tests and get back to me right away. I asked him to do a proper chain of custody so the samples could be used in court if necessary.

Each one will be untouched except by him; each will be labeled with the date and time and kept after the results are documented. I asked him to look for any dangerous compound; in fact, anything out of the ordinary."

"Thanks, Ted. I don't know what we could have done without your involvement or your friends," said Harv. Tory piped in, "We're all anxious to learn the results." Walt nodded in affirmation.

While they ate, Harvey told them about his night. He talked again about his conversation with Brenda to bring Ted up-to-date and then of his 2:15 a.m. event, thanking Ted for the door lock also. As he told them that the nurse was on break at that time, they all agreed with Harv that the person who tried to get into Harv's room knew it and would have tried to do Harvey some sort of harm. Also, Harv mentioned that he had not received a copy of the official complaint he had made. They agreed that Culpepper would not allow it to go through to corporate.

Ted had done his research briefly this morning about who they might ask to get involved in the investigation. Ted said that the right organization was the Illinois Department of Public Health. They had more than 1,200 facilities on the books serving over 100,000 residents from the young to the elderly. Ted also said that the department helped Medicare and Medicaid to certify the facilities for federal payment and reimbursement programs. If Wildstone lost that, it would mean total collapse for them. The Illinois Bureau of Long-Term Care was responsible for ensuring that homes complied with the state's Nursing Home Care Act. Ted said, "Knowing this now, my next step is to call my paper and find out if we have any trustworthy contacts in either department who can make this investigation a priority and get it working right away. My concern is that if we report it by just going through normal channels, it may linger way too long." Everyone was jotting notes and nodding as he spoke. Just as Walt was going to say something, Ted's phone rang. He listened intently as he took down some notes. Into the phone, he finally said, "Yes, Mike. I know you must report this. Please put the call off as long as you can because it will alert Wildstone to what we're doing. Use my name and explain that we don't want them going to Anthony Culpepper yet until they've spoken with us. Call me back and let me know. Thanks."

With a sad look, Ted got off the phone. "Well, we know," he said. "Both the syringe and the food are full of Potassium

Chloride. The liquid in the syringe ground-up pills in the food." "So, what does that mean," asked Walt.

Ted took a moment to gather his thoughts. He was affected by what he had just heard. He then spoke. "This is a big deal," he said. "Mike Wynch, my friend, the chemical analysis expert, told me that both the syringe and the food tested positive for significant doses. It could not have gotten there accidentally. It was very intentional. The liquid in the syringe would have likely been fatal, and the amount in the food could have been fatal or crippling. Using this chemical mimics a heart attack and causes a condition called Hyperkalemia. It is hard to find by testing unless one is specifically looking for it. Without knowing Potassium Chloride has poisoned someone, it's rarely detected, and the victim is dead! As you heard, I asked Mike to put off reporting this to the authorities as long as he can so we can have the opportunity to gather more evidence before Culpepper and Bilford are notified. They have already probably thought about how to cover their tracks!"

Tory mentioned that she thought it was great that there was now proof, and it was exciting. Harv spoke up and said, "That's all fine and good, but I need to find proof that

Culpepper and maybe Bilford were the ones responsible for taking everything that was mine and putting me into a situation where I can't leave." Walt piped in, "That's not true, Harv! I have been researching …Wildstone cannot keep you here if you're of sound mind and body. You can tell them you are going to leave. They will probably make a stink, but you can sign out 'AMA,' which is 'Against Medical Advice.' They can fight it only by proving that you do not have the capacity physically or mentally. But you have plenty of proof that you are indeed capable."

Tory retorted, "But we can't do that now until this case is resolved. Besides, without getting his money and home back, where is Harv going to go, and how will he afford it? We need Harvey to lead this team to a successful conclusion!"

Finally, Harvey spoke. "You are right, Tory. Even if I could walk out of here right now, I would not. You folks are too important for me to walk out; plus, we must get Culpepper and at least Bilford out of here and into jail cells. We are not sure anyone else was involved who knew about their crimes, but they must pay the piper. I'm not so sure that Wildstone had anything to do with it, but they have responsibility for what has happened to me and perhaps others without their knowing. I'm sticking around unless it makes sense for me to leave, and then I'll still end this mystery!"

"Good man," said Ted. "Good man."

Evidence to Demand a Verdict

The Team talked about what they needed. They finally agreed on a list of evidence necessary to assure them victory over Wildstone, Anthony Culpepper, and Charles Bilford. What they had already included; Harvey's loss of money and property; the break-in to Harvey's room and the attempt to get his evidence; the tainted syringe and meal; the listening in through the intercoms; confirmation of Anthony Culpepper's presence in the corridor just before the break-in; Brenda's cautions and other "hearsay" evidence. They agreed that what they needed included copies of the documents providing Power of Attorney to manage or dispose of Harvey's assets; evidence of where the assets had gone; direct witnesses or proof like fingerprints of Culpepper's or Bilford's involvement in any of the items above; and, any collaboration from others who directly were asked to participate in some of the wrongdoing.

This was a tall order; they all decided. Ted said that he and a friend from the newspaper would gather evidence from the sale of Harvey's property and belongings, including his money. He said most of the documents could be discovered through the public domain. Harvey and Walt agreed that they would take on digging out the Wildstone witnesses and people. They decided they would speak directly to Adam, Charlene, Linda Pegwell, and anyone else who could have witnessed any conspiracy against Harvey, including listening in to their apartments and rooms through the intercom system.

Ted went off to make a call to his co-investigators from the Globe, and the others remained at the table, deciding the steps to take. The Team, as they now called themselves, agreed that they would need an excellent digital mini tape recorder with good enough quality to identify voices from the recordings. Harvey recommended that they meet with Brenda because he felt Brenda could get the others to speak with the Team. Tory suggested that to protect Brenda and the others; they should all plan a day out and have their witnesses come to them at a venue where they would not likely be seen together. They all agreed.

Ted returned to The Team and was the first to speak. "My co-investigator at the Globe is in!" Ted sounded excited. "His name is J.B. James. He reminded me that following the property and investments is relatively easy because the house, the investments, and bank accounts were all in Harv's name with his unique social security number. If necessary, Harv will sign documents giving us access to the docs. This will even work with the titles to his vehicles, but they can only be found if they have been sold and recorded. More difficult to track will be personal belongings because there is no required paperwork to sell them. We hope we can just find them. At that point, Harv jumped in, "In my safety deposit box, if I still have it, I have a thumb drive with photos of all of the rooms in my house that I took for any potential insurance or fire claim. There are some perfect and detailed photos of the more expensive items like the artwork and Margaret's Tiffany lamps." "Excellent" said Ted and asked Harvey if he had the key. Harvey at first said that he did not, but then remembered that because he lived alone, there was one in a dresser drawer in the bedroom, but he had asked Neil Goldman at Veteran's Bank if he would keep one of the two keys for Harvey in the event it was needed. A joyful "Ahhhhh" came from the lips of The Team simultaneously. Harv said, "Until now, I hadn't thought about the safety deposit box but let's go to the bank and look through it. Maybe there are other things we can use like the original invoices describing the Tiffany lamps and artwork. It might help us." They all agreed.

It was approaching 4:00 p.m., and there was ample time to go to the bank and then to the office supply store to pick up a useful digital recording device. They all piled into Ted's rental car, and off they went.

Upon arriving at the bank, Neil saw Harvey and trotted from his office to the lobby to greet him. "Harv, it's so good to see you. I was pleased to get your phone call and now to see you. Are these folks with you?" Harv responded affirmatively and asked if they could meet in Neil's office. They went in and shut the door.

Harv took the lead. "Neil, what we are going through right now is of vital importance and secrecy." He introduced The Team and their backgrounds and how they were working together. "Neil, we are trying to gather untainted evidence that my money, property, and belongings were stolen. I need to get into my Safety Deposit Box, and the only key available will be the one that I gave you for safekeeping. Do you still have it? And did anyone else try to get into the box?"

Neil said that he didn't know if anyone else had tried. Still, he would have their security team look through the videos starting with the week that the Power of Attorney was submitted through the week after transferring the property, and monies were accomplished. He thought it might take some time, but it could be done. Neil then said, "Harv, I have the key." He rummaged through his desk drawer, pulled out an envelope, and handed Harvey the key. He said, "First, you'll have to sign the signature card. Let's go get your box and, if you want, you folks can use my office to go through the contents." The Team thanked Neil, then Harv and Neil went back to retrieve the box. After bringing the box to Neil's office, Neil left to do some other things while they used his office.

As Harvey opened the box, he quickly retrieved the thumb drive and pulled it out. They then watched on as he went through the essential papers. They talked about it and separated the deeds for Harv's house and the titles for his truck and mustang. He also had copies of the closing documents for the home, which showed his signature clearly when he bought the house. There were the bills of sale, just like Harv had said, for the three original Tiffany lamps, a desk lamp and other things that Margaret had purchased from Larry Zinzi, an outstanding Tiffany dealer in New York, and some of the fine artwork that Margaret had bought at a show in Chicago. They felt these were important to show that Harvey had owned them and their values at the purchase time. One of the problems with personal property is to prove that a lamp or painting belonged to you rather than the person in whose possession it was. All the lamps were initially numbered, and the numbers were on the bills of sale. When Neil returned, they asked if he would make them copies of the documents because they sure didn't want to lose them! After making the copies, Harv had Neil notarize each as a "correct copy" of the paper. They then placed the originals into the box and returned it to the vault. Harvey kept the thumb drive. They would look at it later using Walt's or Ted's computer.

Upon finishing at the bank, they headed for the Office Depot, where Harv could find a small but excellent digital recorder. He bought it, and they returned to the car. Ted suggested, "It's been a long day. Why don't we get some Chinese take-out and bring it to Tory's to eat? We could eat at the restaurant, but if we stay gone too long when it's not our habit, it may be noticed." They all agreed, and off to The Rainbow Garden on South Neil, they went.

Armed with some sesame chicken, beef and Chinese vegetables, lemon chicken, sweet and sour pork, and plenty of fried rice and egg rolls, they headed back to Wildstone. Ted suddenly switched lanes and turned right on red, which was allowed. He then made another right turn back into the plaza where the restaurant was located, then back onto the same boulevard where they were before. "Sorry, folks. Don't think I'm crazy, but I thought we were being followed. Either I lost them with my crazy moves, or I imagined things. I'm just a little paranoid. I didn't see anybody trying to keep up with us when we did our crazy turnaround." They all laughed, and Tory told Ted that it was the most exciting car ride she'd had in years.

In a few moments, they arrived back at Tory's. When they went inside, they checked the intercom and heard nothing at all. "Being monitored," Ted whispered. So, they all spoke in familiar voices about sitting down to eat and sharing their different dishes. That is until Walt took a small pillow and taped it over the intercom. Then they felt more comfortable. They were enjoying dinner when Tory's doorbell rang. Walt was about to answer it when Tory rolled over in her wheelchair and pulled the pillow off the intercom. At the door was a maintenance man who said, "I'm checking all of the intercoms to make sure they're working correctly. We had a report that yours might have some problems." His name tag said, "Stephen," and Walt wrote it down. He went over to the intercom, put a tester to it, pressed the red button, and told them it seemed to be working. Then off he went and back onto the intercom went the pillow.

Harv said, "I think that Culpepper's getting frustrated that he can't listen in to us and sent Stephen over. We'll have to question Stephen too." They agreed and wrote it on their list. They finished the much-appreciated different cuisine and then talked about how they should proceed. The Team's rules were cast first.

They agreed they would not break the law but would go right up to the line. They would not assume anything and would get evidence of anything they suspected or knew outright that was wrong. Their evidence would include witness reports, tape recordings, interview notes, photographs, and copies of essential papers and documents. If something that was not photographed, recorded, or documented, they would get others who would witness their observations. Once they had their case, then the authorities would be brought in. They would have invested too much to do a sloppy job. Ted helped them realize the importance of real evidence.

How would they possibly get others from Wildstone to speak with them? They agreed that they would set a date and then ask Brenda to "invite" John, Charlene, Neil, Andrea, Adam, Glenda, Mike, and Stephen to speak with The Team at a convenient location away from Wildstone. They would use Harv's new recorder to record each interview and then put together the data. If they were thorough, they could involve both the Illinois Dep't of Health and the Illinois State Police, Division of Criminal Investigations (DCI). None of The Teams could afford to become a target!

Collecting

The next morning, after another day of the boys exercising to Billy Banks and becoming lighter, stronger, faster, and with better balance and stamina, they proceeded with no problems to clean up and head to Tory's for some planning.

The Team met inside due to some rain. As usual, they first checked the intercom, and it was safe to speak. Harv was pleased that Tory had made some fresh coffee, of which he felt in great need. Their first discussion was to ask Harv to call Brenda and convince her to contact those they wanted to speak with. Harvey did so, and Brenda said she would do it and that she would be at work tomorrow and would come to see Harv and get the list of people, the place, and times.

"That's great," said Ted. "Now, we must make our list in order of those with whom we want to talk and then find a place so we can invite them." "That's good," said Tory, "and the place we choose should be easy to get to and close enough not to cause a problem for anybody while being completely private." "That may be hard to find," said Walt. "What about Veterans Bank?" asked Harvey. Neil will be willing and able to get us his private conference room. Also, nobody would be suspicious of someone going to the bank, and it's only a few blocks from here. Some of our 'witnesses' probably bank there. If you agree, I'll call Neil." In a few more moments, Harv got off the phone and said, "Day after tomorrow; that's when the conference room is free all day. Neil said he'd provide cold water in pitchers and some glasses, but if we want coffee or soft drinks, we'll have to provide them."

Everyone agreed. Now all they had to do was determine in what order they would conduct the interviews. They were all avoiding the word "interrogation." Ted suggested that they interview them in the order in which they appeared in action, but Tory made a good point. "It's more important to get them in here when they can make it, so let's try to schedule them in order, but we will be pleased to see them at the time they can best make it." With agreement by all, then Harvey spoke. "I think it is vital that no person sees the other coming out of the bank, or they will be concerned. Let's make sure we schedule them for up to one hour at one hour and twenty-minute intervals. That way, we can complete and consolidate our notes, have a little discussion, take a break if necessary, and then be ready for the next person. We also need to make sure we're right on time to prevent them from running into one another." All agreed, and Walt said, "We can even tell them that we have concerns for their privacy, and therefore they should leave the bank right away after our sessions." "Good point, Walt," Ted said.

"So, who do we have to see?" asked Tory. "Probably more than we'll get to come to see us!" said Ted. Harv mentioned that if they could, John the P.T., Andrea Carlin from Jensen Securities, Neil from Veterans Bank, and others who were not believed to be complicit in Culpepper's scheme might have some insight that could be worthwhile. Walt and Tory both said that indeed Adam, who tried to use the syringe on Harvey, Linda Pegwell, who he caught going through his room, Glenda the Duty Nurse, and Charlene should be spoken with, and they all agreed. Ted reminded them that Stephen, the intercom technician, might have some information. Tory mentioned that Charlene, if she decided to speak to them, would likely be the most unwilling, especially if she was somehow involved. Ted said, "We have to be careful with Charlene because if she's involved with Culpepper, she'll go right back to him and tell him what we're doing." That was in synch with everyone's thinking, and so they would consider how to speak with her. After all, The Team was all seniors except for Ted.

They made their list, and Harv would pass it to Brenda the next day for the calls to begin!

Ted had gone to the supermarket and picked up a cold cut and veggie trays for lunch. It was quite tasty. "Why eat all of Tory's food?" he asked. Once they had eaten and heard of some of Ted's past interesting investigations, Ted's phone rang. He went out onto the patio to take the call. The rest of the group was waiting to use Walt's or Ted's computer to review the flash drive with the pictures of Harv's house and belongings when Ted came back in. He looked thunderstruck! The Team urged him to tell them what happened. He sat down and said, "We struck gold! J.B. found the actual document files for the deed to your house Harv, the title to your truck and the mustang, and the transfer of your investments and savings account. Harvey, that you signed the docs giving J.B. access to the information and had it notarized helped. J.B. mentioned that Neil was accommodating to provide his information. He has requested certified copies of the documents and asked to ensure that all the signatures were perfectly legible to compare them. Neil was especially helpful because he found he can go through the bank's video for the day of the transactions and see who came to the bank 'on your behalf.'" We're closing in, and Culpepper doesn't even know it." Harvey was pleased but not ecstatic. "I know this is great news, but I know my home has been sold, and it's gone. And my belongings, Margaret's beautiful artwork, and lamps and my Mustang are gone and belong to somebody else now. The best I can hope for is to get my money back either from Culpepper, Bilford, or a lawsuit at Wildstone." That's tough, agreed the Team.

"Should we go to the police now?" Tory asked. Harvey said, "I don't think so; not yet. We need all the evidence we have now and the recordings from our interviews to come. We're very confident that we've got Culpepper and Bilford but don't yet know others who may be involved." "I think Harv's right," said Ted. "All of my investigative experience tells me the more proof, the better. But we're getting very close. Besides, if we bring the police in now, they'll take over the investigation, and we won't have any say in who they speak with and what they ask them." Everyone agreed with Ted.

The next step was to put together the interviews. Their list included John the Physical Therapist, Andrea from Jensen Investments; Neil from Veterans Bank; Adam from Memory Care who tried to force the shot on Harvey; Linda Pegwell who went through Harv's room; Charlene from Mr. Culpepper's office; Glenda the Duty Nurse and Stephen, the intercom technician. Harvey agreed to call Brenda at home this evening to share the list rather than risk doing it while Brenda was at work.

Harvey's cell phone rang. It startled him because the only people who would call him were there with him, and he didn't regularly receive calls. It was Neil Goldman from Veterans Bank. He sounded excited! "Harv, Harv, I've got something!" he excitedly spoke. "Security was able to match the date of the withdrawal of your funds to a videotape, and it's clear! It's that lawyer himself, Charles Bilford. He presented the Power of Attorney and received a cashier's check for the total amount! We've got him!" Harv was shocked but not surprised. "They didn't feel the need to protect their identities because they never in a million years thought I would survive!" he replied. "Can you somehow email me a copy of the video?" "Negative," said Neil. "But I'll put it on a thumb drive, and you can pick it up." "Great, Neil. Thanks. You'll also need to get copies of the docs. I will want them, and you can be sure the police will want them too!" Harvey was visibly pleased. "One of The Team will pick them up later today!" he said.

The others paid rapt attention while hearing Harv's side of the conversation. As he explained, they all felt some elation as their proof came out. Ted said, "I'll call and find who the police here use for handwriting and forgery analysis. We need to be ready to go with that document and those we should receive tomorrow from J.B. Wow! We're going to win this. We can prove that the docs are forgeries and that Bilford and Culpepper were the bad actors; we win." Tory chimed in, "It looks like we have proof of Bilford's involvement, but do we have actual proof of Culpepper's guilt other than common sense?" Walt said, "I think we will after the interviews." "Let's hope," said Harv.

"I think it's time to look at the photos on Harvey's thumb drive," said Ted as he opened his laptop. Everyone crowded around as Ted brought up the pictures. There were many! As he clicked through the pictures slowly, Harvey made some comments about a couple of Rembrandt prints that had lots of value, other specific artwork, and three original Tiffany Lamps ...a "Tyler Scroll" in blue, a "Dogwood" and a large, 24" round "Rosebush." They were very highly valued. Then, of course, there were several excellent photos of Harvey's '65 red Mustang. They all commented on how nice Harvey's condo was and the beauty of the artwork and lamps. Harv reaffirmed Margaret's taste in those investments. Tory said that those items should be identified if they were found and that the Mustang would undoubtedly have a title. They all agreed but also realized that if they were sold off, they would have no idea where they were. Harvey interjected that his photos, framed and otherwise, of Margaret and their memories together would be hard to replace. They also realized that Harvey's request to track down his social security payments and pension could take some weeks to receive and understand; after all, they would move at the speed of government! Even with the progress, this wasn't easy. It was an exciting chase, but not easy!

Harvey excused himself to call Brenda. She answered on the third ring. Harv asked her if she could make calls tonight to get appointments set for the day after tomorrow. He explained that they were going to protect those who came from being identified and, therefore, to schedule them at one hour and twenty-minute intervals. It was essential that one would not run into another at the bank. Brenda agreed and said she'd catch up with Harv tomorrow about her progress. With great appreciation, Harv ended the call. Harv then told the others that Brenda would start calling people. "We're close to having this case solved," said Walt. "Once we can get the documents that were used to steal your stuff and prove that they were forgeries and, from the interviews, get some more evidence of Culpepper and Bilford trying to stop us from finding out, combined with Mike Wynch's chemical analysis showing the poison in the syringe and the food, we win!" Tory said, "Let's not put the cart before the horse yet. We've got to finish strong and then go to the police." They all agreed, but not without feeling a little victorious. Ted headed off to the bank to pick up the thumb drive and documents from Neil. The rest of The TEAM thought about the questions they should ask of each person who agreed to be interviewed. Some of their questions were:

What about Harvey's situation at Wildstone did you know?

How did you hear about it?

From whom?

Who asked you to do what you did?

Did he/she tell you why?

How did you feel about doing what you did?

If not mentioned earlier, do you think Mr. Culpepper/others were involved?

Why did you think they were involved?

163

What did you tell them?

Harvey has learned that everything he worked for, house, cars, money, have been taken from him since he's been here. Who do you think could be responsible? Why?

Naturally, there would be other questions that would come up based upon what the person had to say, but these were the most important to ask. In the meantime, Ted returned with the thumb drive and the documents. "Let's see them right away," exclaimed Tory with an excited tone! The others all agreed. They first looked at the Power of Attorney paperwork submitted to the bank with a fake letter of intention supposedly from Harv. It was not so evident that they were forgeries. "Someone practiced very hard to get this pretty close," said Ted. Then they looked at the copies of the safety deposit box sign-in card that Bilford must have signed to try to get into the box and retrieve deeds and auto titles. Harv said, "He got the deeds and other documents from the courthouse because he couldn't get into the box." Harv's forged signature was the product of someone, but not necessarily Bilford. This was ample evidence. Now they would soon receive more documents from J.B. James that would put nails in the coffin. Plus, the interview results could give them some useful information. "I'm hoping that J.B.'s info can tell me where to find my money and then get back my social security and pension too!"

Walt said, "I think we'll be likely to get it restored, but it may take some time and legal action to get it back. Then you'll have to shop for a new house and furniture!" Harv nodded in agreement. "This sucks," he said. "And I'm overcome by thoughts of how this may have happened in times before to unsuspecting, not so savvy residents or those who have dementia or other critical illnesses. We have to make sure that we can help them!" Ted said, "Do you mean The Team won't 'retire' once we get your life back, Harv?" "After learning how to do this and investigate? I sure hope we're not done!" said Harv. The rest of The Team nodded in sincere agreement!

Back in his room later than night, Harv was both reviewing the day's happenings and trying to anticipate who might come tomorrow. His phone rang, and as he picked up, Brenda quickly identified herself. She wanted to talk about how her calls went to the people on the list. She first said that everybody was suspicious of sitting in a room answering questions. Brenda said, "I assured everyone that we were attempting to find out who had taken your assets and that their opinions were of much value. I told them that it's not like an interrogation, but a discussion of their opinions and observations. Most of them accepted, and even Charlene will be there! She's anxious that Mr. Culpepper will find out. I assured her that he would not." She told Harv the order in which the people would be there, and she had promised they'd all be right on time. Harv said, "Well, Brenda, the stage is set, largely because of your help and your good reputation among the other employees. Thank you so much." Brenda told Harv he was welcome and wished him good luck. While Harv later thought about it, he had never really told Brenda about The Team and their organized investigation. It was going to be a big and important day! Harvey set his new lock and prepared for bed.

The Uncovering

The Team met for an early breakfast at Tory's of scrambled eggs, toast, and fruit before they headed to the bank for their day of interviews. They had to be there before 8:00 a.m. to begin on time. They had decided to do the eight interviews, if they all showed up, for one-hour apiece and then have 20 minutes to complete notes, take bathroom breaks or eat something throughout the day. It would be a long day! The 20 minutes of downtime would also help to prevent one person from running into the next. At 7:30 a.m., they piled into Ted's rental car and drove the short distance to the Bank. Once at Veterans' Bank, they were shown to the room. They prepared the table for the interviews and put the food and drinks in the small refrigerator. Harvey took the digital recorder, and it was quickly hidden in a decorative flowerpot in the center of the table. It would be started just before each interview and stopped upon its conclusion. Each person would be told that he/she was being recorded and asked for their verbal permission. They had brought extra batteries and a spare memory card... Harv told the others not to get so excited that they spoke over one another or sounded like they were

167

accusing the person of being a bad actor. Harvey also explained that rather than be accusatory and make them seem guilty, he would tell each person that during his time at Wildstone, he had several situations where he felt someone was watching and listening to him. He would even admit to the break-in of his room. He would also tell them that he had discovered that his money had been embezzled. Then he would ask them if they could help him think through what might have happened. He advised The Team just to use follow up questions like, "How did you get involved?" or "What did you think about it?" or "When that happened, what did you do next?" They all agreed that only by being receptive would people speak openly.

The interviews went well for the most part. John Moran, the P.T., had no knowledge beyond helping Harv become physically capable again, much less ordered a shot for Harvey. Andrea from Jensen Securities, like Neil at Veterans' Bank, would search the videos, but she believed that several documents conducted their transactions, so the video was unlikely. Andrea also stated with no reservations that Harvey had been very dedicated to his investments and was shocked when she saw them liquidated. She said she had worked with J.B. to provide copies that Harv should see very soon. Glenda, the Duty Nurse, had little to add. She knew, of course, that Harv had some problems but didn't know anything except that Mr. Culpepper had been in the corridor one evening. The Team was a bit frustrated that so many had shown up to speak, but no real information was forthcoming. Then things changed!

Adam, the Nurse/Orderly from the memory care unit, admitted that he felt awful about the run-in with Harv and Walt, especially that it became a physical confrontation. When asked how it all happened, Adam recalled that his boss and head of the Memory Care Unit, Chris Blanner, had given him the syringe and told him that John had ordered it to help Harv advance more quickly. Mr. Blanner had insisted that the shot had to be delivered, no if's, and's or but's, and it would be bad for Adam if it didn't happen. Of course, when asked who Blanner worked for, it was Anthony Culpepper! Adam did say that Mr. Blanner was livid when he heard that Adam had failed in his attempt.

Next, there was a short interview with Stephen, the intercom technician. He expressed significant distress at what had happened to Harv. When asked how he was contacted to check the intercom in Walt's apartment, he said that Charlene had called in the work order. There was nothing wrong with the intercom, and he filed the maintenance report as such. A pattern was building that Mr. Culpepper was very much involved with this situation. But it was all speculation; The Team was looking for evidence!

Linda Pegwell did not come but sent a short message to the bank that her schedule had changed. The Team had what they needed in that Linda had admitted when Harv caught her in the room that Mr. Culpepper himself said he would pick up the syringe. They also thought that Harv's "openness" to let her see everything in his place had helped defuse the situation.

Then, their last interview of the day was to be explosive!

Surprisingly, Charlene Rogers, Mr. Culpepper's secretary, had agreed to speak with The Team. She was very concerned about her confidentiality and had asked if she could come late in the day. She presented herself at about 4:30 in the afternoon. As usual, when Charlene took a seat at the table, she projected the character of one who was righteous, in charge, and would be resistant to answer questions. She said she only came to see what this was all about. As she sat on the edge of her chair, with her back very straight, Harv took a chance.

He said, "Charlene, thank you so much for coming. You, more than anyone, are likely to have more information about what has happened to me. You see, Charlene, as I emerged from 5 months of being in a coma and began to slowly get better with the help of all the good people at Wildstone, I began to wonder about my assets and home, as I'm sure you can understand. And, as you have, I had scrimped and saved to start my company and provide a good life for my wife and me. Once she died, I had no more interest in my company and sold it and our home and moved to a condo, which I decorated with all our fondest memories. I had also saved for years and sold my company so I could live independently. As my head cleared, I began to check with my banker and investment advisor only to find all; not some, but all of that money was gone. I also found, with the help of others (not naming Walt to keep him from being complicit), that my condo had been sold and the contents gone. Charlene, can you imagine coming out of a fog and learning that? Can you imagine what kind of person might do such a thing? What their families and co-workers would think of them? So, I'm searching to find my assets and those responsible for this considerable theft, directly or as an accessory. Is there anything you can tell me that might help? Please?"

Charlene remained stoic and stern for a few moments while she gathered her thoughts and emotions. She said, "It is horrible what you have gone through. I'm sorry for your struggles and pain. But I have no knowledge that would help ..." She stopped mid-sentence and had to compose herself and then, all of a sudden, with no warning, broke into great sobs as her body convulsed with grief and guilt. The Team was shocked. It was undoubtedly nothing they had expected, and her past and even initial behavior this day had her pegged as a tough and unemotional woman. She had a moral compass and feelings too!

Harvey gave her a bottle of water and a box of tissues that were in the room. They all gave her the moment to compose herself and then told her that they were very interested in what she would have to say. Once she calmed herself, things came forth. She told them that she expected this to be a problematic hour and had taken the following day off to keep from seeing Mr. Culpepper. She first described their relationship. Early on, ten years prior, when Charlene took the job, she admired him. He was a strong leader and was always in charge. She took pride in working for the top executive at Wildstone Champaign. Over time, he began to trust her with his ideas and plans for the facility. Sometimes, he was overly dictatorial, and more and more, he seemed to care not about those they served, the residents, but more about what he wanted. It seemed like even the Board of Directors should only do what Anthony Culpepper suggested. Charlene said that over the last several years, there was considerable turnover on the Board, but that Charles Bilford and Mr. Culpepper became tight friends and even met about once weekly. She said it was as though they were strategizing the future for the Senior Living Community. Through her tears, Charlene admitted that sometimes, her best defense was to put up an image of unapproachability, which kept people away. It also meant she didn't have to explain herself. The Team thought she was opening up! Then came the most important information!

Charlene, through her conversations with Mr. Culpepper, her preparing correspondence for him, and her overhearing conversations in the office, had damning evidence. She started by telling The Team that he seemed rattled when Brenda, the Charge Nurse for Harv, reported that Mr. England was awakening, and she and the others were shocked. Mr.

Culpepper set out for Mr. England's room to see what was happening. She thought that was odd because he seldom seemed to care about the status of any individual patient or resident. She also recalled that when he returned to his office, he felt insulted by Mr. England and even asked me if I thought his suit was nice! Charlene went on, speaking to Harvey. "As you became better and better, he became more and more agitated. He was distraught when you and Mr. Schell began to work out and become physically strong. I remember his yelling at Chris Blanner, who runs Memory Care, about failing miserably at a simple task he was asked to do." Charlene talked about hearing Mr. Bilford and Mr. Culpepper talking about trying to keep Mr. England in "the dark" but didn't know what about. She also remembered that both men spent some time in the audio room where the public address system and the intercoms were located. They even had her call in a work order for Mr. Schell's intercom because it wasn't working. Charlene had been there longer than she agreed to and was still very emotional. She said, "Are you sure you will not tell Mr. Culpepper that I was here?" Harvey told her that he would not say a thing but that the police or other authorities like the Illinois Department of Public Health and the Department of Long-Term Care might be interested in speaking with her. He also correctly told her that it was also illegal for her to be fired or harassed as retaliation for her testimony. She was still uneasy as she prepared to leave.

Harv had another quick thought. He asked her if she had ever been to Mr. Culpepper's house. She said she had been there a couple of months ago for a birthday party for his wife. Charlene also said she went only because declining would have been an insult to Mr. Culpepper. Harv asked her to describe his house, which she said was very large, in a beautiful neighborhood. Pulling out Walt's laptop, Harv inserted the thumb drive and opened up his pictures of his house and asked her to review them for anything familiar quickly. She quickly scanned the photos and mentioned that several things looked amazingly similar to stuff in the Culpepper's home. She focused on the stained-glass lamps and said he was bragging to the men about his '65 mustang. Some other artwork looked familiar, she said, but she wasn't sure. At that moment, not only Harvey but The Team all knew this was what they had been waiting for. Although they would talk about it later, it was a significant moment!

The Team realized that this recording would be a prize and would be likely to be turned over to the police. The interviews had been a success, and the tapes would be proof. The only additional explanations they wanted were the forged document copies used for the transfer and sale of Harv's assets. Those would come from J.B. very soon!

As they said their goodbye's to Charlene, with additional assurances that Mr. Culpepper would not hear about her comments until it was necessary, she was emotionally and physically worn out.

The team huddled together for a few minutes after their last interview. "Wow," said Walt. "This was amazing. We not only have all the circumstantial evidence from others, but Charlene's interview gave us lots!" Tory chimed in, "You're right, Walt. This was worth it. I hope the recorder got everything perfectly. Not only should we check it, but we need to duplicate the tape and keep a copy here in a safety deposit box. If we lose the tape, we lose everything!" Ted slipped out to ask Neil if he had any equipment to duplicate the tape. He returned to the room and said, "Neil has the equipment to duplicate the digital recording. He will bring it in right away." Neil was in the conference room in a few minutes, showed them how to dupe the tape, and they had made two copies within a short time. They listened to each to make sure they captured everything. Very encouraged, they had Neil provide signature cards for access to Harv's Safety Deposit Box and placed the original and one copy in the box. As before, Neil kept the safety deposit box key. It would be much safer that way. They took one copy of the tape with them. Things were looking good so far. J.B. was supposed to be bringing his evidence tomorrow, so they were in good spirits. They were all tired and hungry, so agreed to go to the Olive Garden for dinner.

It had been a productive day!

Trying to Obstruct

While The Team was headed to dinner, Anthony Culpepper and Charles Bilford sat in Culpepper's office after hours. They felt more comfortable with the rest of the staff in the offices gone. Both were worried about keeping themselves out of the story. They somehow knew something was up... They knew that Harvey had caught Linda Pegwell searching his room; they knew that Harv had to know the "key to his house" was missing, and they knew that Adam had overtly failed in his attempt to give Harv the shot of "B12". They also discussed that most every day was spent with Walt Schell and Tory Randall, not to mention her nephew Ted. Bilford said, "So how much do you think they know? And what do they know?"

Culpepper replied, "They know just what we talked about. England must know by now that his money and home are gone, and he's probably trying to figure out why. He's got some other money that we didn't know about because he doesn't seem overly concerned about it. That's unfortunate because he isn't limited to our grounds and, with his buddies, can get out and about without restrictions. He really cannot have anything against us. Let's face it; they are all old folks without any investigative skills, and they wouldn't know where to find any evidence. And, I'm sure England hasn't called the police because the Chief of the Champaign PD is a friend of both of ours."

"You know, Anthony, you may be right, but how do we keep them from doing anything? England has lost way over a million with his home, furnishings, car, and bank accounts. He will work hard to get it back. The trail, if followed, will lead right back to Wildstone and then you and me. So how do we prevent any trail from developing? We do not want evidence leading to us. We could do decades in prison. The shortfalls in Wildstone's budget before we used England's money to cover us would show embezzlement charges on top of what we did to England. If only the doctors were right and he had died, we would have no problems. Are you sure he doesn't have anything?" asked Charles.

"Of course, I can't know for sure, but I don't think so," said Anthony. "Besides, if England had gone to the police, we would know, and there would be a long investigation with warrants for records and such. There is not much more they could know except that his wealth is gone. He would have to

179

go to the cops. I'm a little concerned because even with checking on the intercoms, they have not provided anything. We haven't been able to hear a thing!"

Bilford chimed in, "I think that if there's any chance they do know, and we let them report it, we could be in big trouble. Is there any way we can do something? Maybe using England's medication? Think maybe a heart attack, stroke, dementia, etc.? And do you have those types of meds in stock so we wouldn't have to raise suspicions by ordering them?"

"It's worth a shot," replied Culpepper. "I agree. We need to act rather than just hope he doesn't cause a rat's nest. Besides, if he gets sick or even dies, there's nobody to miss him. That was part of the appeal to us. He was alone, no heirs we know about, had lots of cash and investments, and a nice home. Plus, he was going to die. Who would know or care once he is gone? Whether its dementia or death, he needs to be out of the way! His new friends would mourn him, but what can they do? They are all old folks whose time has come and gone. I'll check into substances that we might have that could cause the right effects but are hard to trace. If we do not cover ourselves, I think we'll regret it!"

"I agree," said Charles. "I can also put a couple of my firm's investigators on it to intimidate them. Let's go have a drink!"

What They Don't Know

The next morning, Walt and Harv worked out; as usual, when Harvey received an unusual voicemail message. It was from Charlene, and she sounded panicked! She said it was very urgent and to call her back right away and make sure only his friends were present.

Both Walt and Harv decided that it was better to take the call outside in one of the courtyards, so they exited the building called Charlene. When she answered, she asked, "Are you OK? Have you seen Mr. Culpepper or Mr. Bilford this morning? Don't eat anything or take any medication. I'll meet you at the Veterans' Bank at 9:45; be there! It's so important. Bring your recorder. And, if you can, bring Brenda!"

They agreed to meet her there, so they returned to their places to shower and change quickly. On the way, they called Tory to find out if Ted was available to drive them to the bank. He was. Once back at his room, Harv got cleaned up, dressed, and ready quickly. He then had the duty nurse, Glenda, summon Brenda. Brenda met Harv in the lobby, and they stepped outside to talk. Harvey took a deep breath and, in a very few minutes, told Brenda what they had learned, and that Charlene was desperate to meet them and asked for them to bring Brenda. Brenda started in on Charlene, but Harv stopped her and told her, "We don't have much time, Brenda. Please come and find out with us what she wants. She was our best source for information during our interviews so that she may have something important." Brenda asked, "Why does she want me there?" Harv just said, "Let's find out." Brenda went inside and told Glenda that she would be in a meeting for a while and to call her on her cell if she was needed. Harv and Brenda walked to Tory's. They found Ted, Walt, and Tory waiting. Once they all piled into Ted's rental car, space was tight. They arrived at the bank in six or seven minutes and went in to find Charlene waiting anxiously. They asked Neil if they could use the conference room, but it was busy, so he let them use an assistant's office.

Once they felt safe to talk, Harvey asked Charlene what this was all about. Charlene almost fell apart! "First of all, Brenda, I wanted you to hear me give you an apology. I have mistreated you, and with arrogance you do not deserve. My years with Mr. Culpepper got the better of me, and I have too often echoed his attitude. Please forgive me. Once I am no longer useful to you folks, then I will resign my position. In the meantime, I did something shameful, but I am glad that I did. I put my mini recorder underneath the desk intercom to Mr. Culpepper's office when I left last night and turned on Mr. Culpepper's intercom to my desk. I knew he and Mr. Bilford would be meeting, and I was, let's say, just curious. Well, what I heard was shocking and dangerous, especially to Mr. England."

Charlene asked them to listen carefully and played the recording. Once it was over, nobody said a thing. One could have heard them breathing. Finally, Ted softly said, "This is dangerous. For you, Harv, but even for the rest of us as you heard them talk about us." Walt agreed. Tory said with measured tones, "At this stage, we must assume they will do whatever they can and by whatever means they have to stop Harvey. People die every day in senior homes like this, and they control the information. We need to get you out of here, Harv!"

Brenda finally spoke. "We already know that they tried to poison you, listen to your conversations, search your room, and even come into your room when you were there. Harv, you must leave. You told me you have some money that they didn't find. You need to get an apartment, either rent a car or buy one, and get some new clothes. Don't even go back to your room." Harv asked, "How can I do that? I have nowhere to go and must terminate my stay at Wildstone." Brenda advised, "We should make some plans. I suggest that Ted take you to a nice furnished executive apartment building that big companies use, then to the store for clothes and personal items and then tomorrow to get a car." Ted agreed. He also stated that once Harv was settled, it would be time to go to the Illinois State Police, Division of Criminal Investigations (DCI) with their information, not the local police who could both slow and tell Culpepper about the investigation. He also suggested that once in his place, Harvey should not ever come back to Wildstone because Culpepper and Bilford would have people waiting. Walt interjected that when they gathered at Harv's new place, they should take a cab because they could be followed.

Although all of this seemed a bit cloak and dagger for Harv, he agreed that once reported; he would be in Culpepper's sights quickly. They were also anxious to hear and see what J.B. had come up with. At this point, it was late morning, so Ted suggested they all go to breakfast and discuss suitable apartments for Harv. Brenda said she could not go because of her schedule, so they agreed to drop her off. She swore herself to secrecy, and they asked her to keep an eye on Harv's room.

With Ted driving his rental, they dropped Brenda off across the street, where others would not see who she was with. They waited until she was in the doors. Then they headed to the Bob Evans on N. Neil Street for breakfast. They had been seated and discussing the situation when Walt said, "You know, it just struck me, Harv. You have had your Social Security and Pension that have been automatically deposited into your accounts. You need to contact both Social Security and Brown & Root and redirect your payments to be deposited into a new checking account." Who knows how much they've stolen?"

Tory said, "Great idea, Walt. "And you should use another bank in case they try to find you through Veterans' Bank. The minute they know you're gone, they'll be on the chase. Harv said, "All good ideas, and we'll do them. There's enough time left in the day we may find an apartment, get a new checking account, buy a car and get some clothes today." Ted said, "We'll sure give it a try." Through a particularly good breakfast for which Harv picked up the tab, they all talked about the next steps. They also were so thankful Charlene came forward.

Because it was already around 11:00 a.m., they all got busy. Ted took both Walt and Tory back to Wildstone and helped Tory navigate her wheelchair while thinking about how strong she was. While not as old as Harv and Walt, who were excellent as it was, she was 66 and yet her chair was not seen as being a disability in any fashion. Wow! She was still the sharp woman he knew when he did investigations for her. That also made him think that J.B. would have some info for them even yet today. They'd better get moving!

Ted and Harvey took off. Harv checked to ensure his license was current... great; he had another two years before it expired. He also still had plenty of cash in his wallet. They went directly to Busey Bank at their main building in Urbana. It had been around for years, and it was less likely, even though Urbana and Champaign were considered "twin cities," that people would snoop around at Urbana banks. The offices weren't as convenient in location, but Harvey would have a car soon and be able to get to where he was going. Harvey opened a checking account with a $50,000.00 balance from his old England Projects Closing account, considering he would need money to buy a car. He had Walt's name put on the account also and took a signature card with him to have Walt sign just in case it would become necessary.

From there, they went to Baytowne Apartments just a bit west of Prospect. They went there first because they were highly regarded. Harvey wasn't into apartment living but understood the necessity. During a visit to the office, they encountered some excellent news. Not only was it one of the nicest complexes in the area, after the tour of a two and a three-bedroom unit, Harvey was all in. As they discussed it with the manager on duty, Marilyn, they learned that there was a building on their little "lake" that was populated with mature adults, so it was quiet and secluded, and there happened to be a gentleman who would be willing to sublet his furnished and large two-bedroom unit with a great view and extra wide doors for wheelchair access. When he heard that, thinking of Tory, Harv asked for a tour. As Harv, Ted, and the manager toured the apartment, they found it immaculate, well-furnished, and decorated even down to towels and linens. Harv signed the agreement to lease it starting immediately. The manager said it would take a day or so to do the credit checks. Both Harv and Ted decided to share "some" secrets with Marilyn. They told her briefly of Harv's remarkable recovery from a severe illness and that his home and wealth had been swindled from him while he was in a coma. It was important during the investigation phase not to alert those with the criminal behavior of Harv's whereabouts and that a credit check could be hurtful and leave a paper trail. Harv then offered to give her six months' rent upfront with the first month in cash. Marilyn agreed to that and to protect Harv's identity from anyone trying to find him. Because the rent paid the utilities, it would help to keep his location secretive. With keys in hand, Ted and Harv moved on. Their next stop was Marketplace Mall, where a quick stop at Penny's, Macy's, and Kohl's provided Harv with some additional shoes, underwear, socks, pants, shirts, and sunglasses. They were also able to pick up personal necessities at CVS nearby. They then called Busey Bank and asked for the manager who opened Harv's account. He had agreed to hold off on ordering checks until Harv had his address. Harvey gave him the address of his new apartment, and the checks were ordered.

It was getting late in the afternoon by this time, so Ted took Harv by Champaign Ford City, only a short distance from the apartment, to look at cars. Harv preferred trucks, but he thought that if he were driving his friends Walt and Tory, he should have a mix of performance, reliability, handling, comfort, and space (for Tory's wheelchair). There was an impeccable, 2017 burgundy Ford Edge Titanium that would meet all those needs. It was low mileage with only 21K on the odometer and came with an extended warranty. Harvey settled with the saleswoman, Kelly, for $23,000.00 and gave her one of his bank's counter checks for half the total. He said he would give her another check for the balance when he picked up the car. Ted saw that Harv was keeping her from running a credit check that would naturally lead to Wildstone. She hesitated because the counter check from Busey Bank was not personalized, and Harv's address on his driver's license did not match the new address he told her. They agreed that she would get the car ready, and in the meantime, would check Harv's bank balance. And, Harv offered, he could come with a cashier's check. With that verification, she could have the car ready by late the next morning. Harv thought what significant progress they were making! They then headed back to the bank quickly for a cashier's check. While they were there, Harv also replenished his wallet with cash from his new account.

Ted called Tory and invited her and Walt to have Chinese at Harvey's new apartment. Of course, they accepted. Then Ted took Harv to the apartment to get used to it and put his new things away while fetching the rest of The Team and the food.

Harv enjoyed a more in-depth look at his new apartment. The model was called The Islander, and it had over 1,600 sq. feet of space on two floors. The vast living room would accommodate his friends. The furniture was of excellent quality and comfort, the kitchen was like that found in an upscale home, and the whole thing was roomy and light. He hung up his clothes, put his other stuff in the drawers, and made a mental note of other things he would need; a hat or two, a rain jacket, regular jacket, and he noticed that while there were some paper goods at the apartment, he'd need to pick up more. He thought how convenient it would be when he picked up his car and had some independence. He sat on his patio that overlooked the nice pond, or "Lake" as they called it, and relaxed until the others showed up.

Ted arrived after picking up The Team and, while having seen the new place, enjoyed showing the others around. Harv heard their "oohs" and positive comments as they toured. Everyone was surprised that Harv had found such a place, taken care of his banking, and bought a car already. He was delighted with the apartment for the present. They quickly sat down to eat before the food got cold.

Walt brought up the subject he had mentioned before; Harv needed to get his social security and pension checks transferred to his account, find out where they had been going, and get the money back. Tory, with her investigative knowledge, suggested that Harvey have his lawyer represent him and get the transfers done without having to reveal Harv's address. After Charlene's recording of the Culpepper/Bilford conversation, it was evident that Harv's safety would be in jeopardy if they knew how to reach him. Walt also suggested that the attorney send a registered letter stating that either with or against Dr.'s advice, Harv had moved from Wildstone and would no longer authorize payments of any kind to the senior living community also, that he would send someone to retrieve his belongings and clothes from the room. They all agreed that this was a good idea.

J.B. was going to report to them today, but with all that had happened, he agreed to come over to Harv's at 9:00 a.m. the next morning. The Team decided to meet again at Harv's because it was much safer than meeting at Wildstone. Once Harvey had his car, though, he could probably sneak over to

Walt's or Tory's apartments because they wouldn't know that Harv was driving or what kind of car he had. They were excited to hear what J.B. had to say and to meet him finally!

After everybody left, Harv sat in the Living Room recliner with only a glimmer of light from the kitchen area. He found that he could look out over the pond that had lights and a fountain. It was relaxing as he thought about everything that the team Walt, Tory, and Ted did to help Harvey. They had become remarkably close. Harv wondered how long Ted would be involved with them. He was still younger and had to earn a living and continue his career. He was such a fine addition. Of course, he had worked on investigations for Tory when she was with The Globe and was wonderfully trained and had an excellent reputation. Harv also wondered how much of his money and possessions that he could he get back, knowing that Charlene's pictures should help. He just wanted to be whole again without worry.

Harvey locked the doors, even the security bar on the sliding glass door to the patio and went to bed. On a new mattress with new noises and so many thoughts in his head, it took a while for him to fall asleep. Because he was dog tired, he slept deeply.

Gathering the Rest of the Evidence

Harv awoke at 7:45 a.m., which was late for him. He felt reasonably rested and headed to take a shower. There wasn't quite enough time for him to try out the excellent community health center before everyone else arrived. Harv liked a hot shower with plenty of water pressure and was pleased to find this was great. He shaved, brushed his teeth, and put on some of his new clothes. He then went to the kitchen and made coffee. While it was brewing, he made breakfast consisting of Rye toast and two eggs scrambled. It was then he realized that his blood pressure meds were still in his room at Wildstone. Maybe Brenda could fetch everything from his room and get it to Ted without arousing any suspicion, he thought.

Right at 9:00 a.m., there was a knock on the door. As Harv was putting his plate away, he noticed that the small TV screen on the kitchen wall showed Ted, Walt, Tory, and the fourth person he presumed to be J.B. at the door. Harv liked that security camera! He opened the door and let everyone in.

Ted introduced J.B. James to Harvey. Harv immediately liked him. J.B. was straight forward and well-spoken, although certainly not quiet. He had a lot to say and was anxious to get everyone filled in. Harv offered them all coffee, refilled his cup, and they all sat down.

J.B. began. He told them about his public records search to find out about the sale of Harv's condo. The documents showed that the house had been sold to the Rochelle family, Scott, and Blynn on the 2nd of April. He followed up with the realtor who sold the place to look at the contract. The house was sold for $383,000.00 unfurnished except for the appliances. There was no mention of the furnishings, artwork, or Harv's Mustang. Tory related the pictures that Charlene had of Harv's late wife's Tiffany lamps and her comments about the mustang. J.B. responded that all that could not be checked until the DCI did their work and got a search warrant for Culpepper and Bilson. That would involve their bank accounts, homes, records, etc. That would happen once The Team met with agents after the official complaint was filed. J.B. then said he had checked new titles issued for automobiles, and one for Harv's Mustang had been registered to Anthony Culpepper. That was a "gotcha" moment. The last part was that Harvey's Brown and Root pension and his Social

Security payments continued to go to a checking account in Harv's name, obviously set up by Culpepper and Bilson.

"Why would they do it in my name?" asked Harv. J.B. said, "One cannot reassign their social security payments to another, so they just set up an account in your name, forged the paperwork, and notified both Brown and Root and Social Security of the change of accounts. Of course, Culpepper and Bilson were signatories on the account so they could just take the money. It amounts to about $5,500.00 per month." "With everything else paid for already, I can live on that much with some to spare," said Harv. Next came some interesting information about Wildstone.

J.B. said, "You all know that Wildstone Champaign is one of many such senior living communities across the country. Culpepper and Bilson are simply employees of Wildstone corporate. We must not assume that Wildstone corporate or even anyone else beyond the two of them was involved in this case or are crooked. You can bet that once this comes out, the company will begin to search into the entire Champaign organization and revenue stream." J.B. went on, "The DCI must hear about this first and do a deep dive. Then, when the Champaign Police are notified, it will be too late for them to help cover for any friends. I figure that Culpepper and Bilson must know senior people in the Police Department, the courts, and the city registrar and clerk's offices."

"So how do we get Harv's money and property back?" questioned Walt. J.B. answered him, "It's sadly unlikely that Harv will get back his house or many of his belongings. The good news is that the photos that Charlene has will help find some of the artwork and lamps from the Culpepper's, and those could be seized and returned within a few weeks of seizure and once the courts authorize. The money, on the other hand, will be dragged out through the courts, and it may take years."

"That sucks," said Tory in an unusual direct tone. She suggested that because the money was probably taken to cover a loss or embezzlement at Wildstone, perhaps if Harv approached the President of Wildstone U.S. and offered to keep quiet about the theft if he were to get it all back including the value of his house, they may find it worth their while to avoid a lawsuit and the negative publicity that it would cause. Both Harv and Ted agreed that it was an excellent tact and would not take too long once Culpepper and Bilson had been charged.

J.B. produced three copies of the documents, including copies of the deed to Harv's home, the title to the mustang, and the banking documents for Harv's pension and social security. He suggested that Harv keep one and put the other in his safety deposit box and that he would keep the third just in case. The Team agreed. Harv then told them that he had copies of the originals of those documents in his safety deposit box at Veteran's Bank that could be used to compare signatures. They agreed that those would be great to produce at the appropriate time!

Next, they had to decide when to call in the Illinois State Police, Division of Criminal Investigations (DCI). Both Ted and J.B. opined that it should be very soon because to delay, it would result in the increased likelihood that Harvey and others might be harmed. They also suggested that duplicate copies of the notes, J.B.'s data, and tapes be kept. Tory said that the recordings could not be used in a court because they were obtained without a legal warrant. But they would certainly be heard, and perhaps a D.A. could find a way to use the information. The Team was swimming in data and realizing that the report would be made over the next couple of days.

Ted took everyone home and then returned with J.B. to take Harv to pick up his new car. When they arrived at the dealership, Kelly had the car looking and running like new, and all the paperwork for the title, taxes, registration, and insurance. Harvey had decided to use the dealer for everything because it would be harder to trace. Harv presented the cashier's check for the balance. Kelly had already checked with the bank to make sure Harv was credible. She turned over the keys and even gave Harv a full tank of gas. Ted and J.B. left, and so did Harv; this time in two different cars. It felt so alien for Harv to be driving on his own again. It seemed so long ago. He really enjoyed his new car and the feeling of freedom to go anywhere. As he drove on Prospect Street, he saw the Walmart and turned in to buy some groceries as he had done regularly in the past. It still felt weird about going shopping by himself. He bought quite a lot this day. 90% lean hamburger, pork chops, rib eye steaks, chicken, packaged salad, salad dressing, bread, lunchmeat, cheese, crackers, eggs, margarine, frozen veggies, and some cashews. He even bought some soft drinks, beer, and wine. After paying, he decided to take the groceries home and get the cold things into the refrigerator. As he drove "home," it was still a funny thought to be going "home" to this place. He put the groceries away and sat in the recliner facing the pond. This is way too comfortable, he said to himself as he faded away into a glorious afternoon nap.

Getting His Money Back

The next morning, Harvey awakened to a beautiful day. He slept late (for him) until almost 7:00 a.m. He threw on a pair of athletic shorts, tennis shoes and a T-shirt and went to put the coffee on. He immediately went out his sliding glass doors and onto the patio and began a short workout while the coffee brewed. He started with some slow stretches; arms out to the side and moving back to his left and then slowly to his right. After 12 repetitions, he touched each toe with the opposite arm for six reps. He dropped down and did 20 pushups, then rolled onto his back and did 20 sit-ups. He laid fully back and did 10, 10-second leg lifts. Harv felt much better and stopped knowing that the coffee would be made. It was Sunday, so before coffee, Harv took his keys and walked to the front building in the complex to buy a paper. He came back to his place, poured his coffee, and opened the paper.

Harv was a bit hungry, so boiled two three-minute eggs and toasted a slice of bread. When they were done, he spread Smart Balance on his toast, put the eggs into egg cups and ate slowly, enjoying his breakfast. Shortly after he finished, he got a call from Walt. Harv realized that over the past weeks, they had been spending days together, and it was a bit lonely to be by oneself. Harv asked Walt if he, Tory, JB and Ted wanted to come over for the afternoon. After Walt's affirmative response, Harv told him he would pick them up at one o'clock. Once he hung up, he called right back and told Walt that they should come out to his car rather than chance people seeing Harv and maybe even following him. Walt agreed. Harv finished reading the paper, showered, cleaned up, got dressed and readied himself for the day. Then he headed over to Wildstone.

Once he arrived, he called Walt and told him he was waiting and where to find him. A few moments later, they all piled into Harv's new car. Ted said, "Man, it's nice to have you take me somewhere for once! Nice car, Harv!" Harv said it was nice to have his independence again and took off. On the relatively short drive to Harv's place, they made idle conversation.

Once they arrived, they decided to gather on his patio. They all agreed that it was an excellent place. Harv said that it was great considering it was tastefully decorated and had excellent quality furnishings considering he had nothing to contribute at present. J.B. liked the place, and since he still lived in Boston, he was jealous of the space for the money! Once they sat down, they began to speak about what needed to be done. Tory suggested that Harv needed to sit with his attorney right away and have him formulate three letters. The first needed to go to Wildstone signing Harv out of their care. At that point, Walt suggested that Harv go to his doctor first thing to have his doctor agree that Harv was able to live independently. All decided that was an excellent tact otherwise Culpepper might get an order forcing Harv's return to Wildstone "for his own good". Then Harv needed to have the attorney representing him to send The Dr.'s affirmation of Harv's abilities to live independently also to Wildstone and registered letters to both Brown and Root's pension plan and to Social Security to redirect their payments to Harvey's new bank account.

Next or even simultaneously, the case needed to be written up concisely with the evidence to support it for presentation to the DCI and then ask that investigators come to see Harv and The Team to speak with them. Harvey surprisingly knew a lead agent at the DCI named Nolan Wilburn because England Projects had coordinated the construction of the office in Springfield about ten years ago. Harv agreed to call him.

The Team spent a couple of hours detailing all pertinent information they had obtained including the "tapes" from the interviews and the photos from Charlene. They documented everything from Harv from finding out he had lost everything to Adam trying to inject him to the meal being poisoned to the listening over the intercoms, to Linda Pegwell going through Harv's room, etc. J.B. had produced forged titles and deeds, even a forged title to Harv's mustang. They could even attest that Harv's pension and social security were going to a fake account in Harv's name but with Anthony Culpepper as the signatory. At the end of the conversation, they felt they had significant evidence to inform the DCI .

The process, they all concluded, was that Harv needed to get an appointment with his physician right away, then meet with his attorney to have the letters written, then with certified copies in hand they would meet with the DCI . They hoped that could all happen by the end of the day Wednesday. Culpepper's and Bilson's day of reckoning would happen soon. Harv suggested one more essential thing. Once the letters were sent from the attorney, Culpepper would try anything to get to Harv, Tory and Walt. Harv suggested that once his lawyer said they were sent, Walt and Tory should pack enough things for a week or better and move in with him. He and Walt would use the two bedrooms upstairs, and Tory would use the Murphy Bed in the living room downstairs. Ted and J.B. . would get a motel nearby. Culpepper would want them gone!

As the evening drew near, they wound down the conversation, and Harv loaded up the car to take everyone back to Wildstone. As he dropped everyone off, he said to Walt, "I need to get a look at Culpepper's house. I'll just put his address into the GPS. I'll park a block away or so and just check it out. Wanna come?" Walt was excited and said, "Wouldn't miss it! But wait a minute. I'll go in and get a pencil, paper, a camera and binoculars." Everyone was cautious, but Harv insisted that he was just going to scope it out with no confrontations. "Culpepper doesn't even know what I drive and where I live." Walt came out in a few minutes with his cache. They promised to text the others when they were done, and off they went! The GPS told them that Culpepper's address was in an area called the Trails at Abbey Fields, one of the best neighborhoods. It was in southwest Champaign. It was a lovely community, and the GPS took them right to Culpepper's house. They made mental note as they passed by but didn't slow down. It was still noticeably light outside, and they didn't want to be spotted. They drove around until they could find a place that was not obtrusive to park and remain unseen. As they sat in the car, the Culpepper's arrived at the home, and as they drove into the driveway, the garage doors opened. There it was in the garage; Harv's red Mustang convertible! Harv could hardly sit still. Walt took out his camera and took a telephoto shot of the mustang before the garage closed again. The garage door closed as they must have gone into the house from a garage entrance. Harv used his cell phone camera and took a picture of his watch with the time and date displayed and the house in the background. This was not a wasted trip. They left and headed back to Wildstone. They stopped at the Steak n Shake for dinner. Walt had a double with fries, and Harv had a patty melt also with fries. As they ate, Harvey's phone rang. It was from Brenda. She said, "Harvey, where are you? Everyone here is looking for you. Charlene has been so nice. She called me to tell me to watch out because Mr. Culpepper is sure that I know where you are and is going to ask me. What should I tell him? How about Walt and Tory and their friends (referring to Ted and J.B.)? Will they be questioned or even in danger?"

Harv told Brenda to hold on while he filled Walt in. Then he said, "Brenda, in anticipation that I would be in danger once this case breaks, I have found a great apartment where

I'm now living. I won't tell you now where I am so you can't be put under pressure to lie. But I am safe. Please tell me if you think the others are in danger." Brenda didn't think they were but that Harv could be in grave danger if he returned because Mr. Culpepper had engaged everyone to keep their eyes out for him, especially near Walt and Tory's places. He had told them that Harv was gravely ill again and they should apprehend him to receive treatment if they saw him. Well played, Culpepper, thought Harv. "Brenda, I'm just fine and in great health. Let's keep in touch throughout this adventure. Thanks for telling me. I'll always take your calls. But do not tell anyone at all my phone number. And do not let your phone out of your sight! You are special. Thank you." After hanging up, they ate and discussed the call.

"I'm worried," said Walt. "Culpepper can convince all the employees that he's a good guy and that you are out here somewhere sick and delusional. If someone sees you at the grocery store or buying gas, it could be bad for you. He may even be able to get a warrant for your welfare to have the police bring you in." "I hadn't thought of that," said Harv. "You may be right. We may have to accelerate our plan. When I drop you off, I'll be quick about it. Once they ate, they headed to Wildstone where Harvey quickly dropped Walt off at the building before his and Walt walked quickly home while Harv left.

The Team Goes to the Authorities

It was Monday 6:42 a.m., and Harv was up and about. As usual, he put on the coffee and went onto the patio to stretch out and do some exercises, including push-ups and sit-ups. He then decided to run the circumference of the complex until he put in about a mile. He felt good and healthy. After a small breakfast and coffee, he took a nice shower while thinking about organizing his day.

Once he was dressed and shortly after 8:30 a.m., Harv put in a call to his physician and friend Tom Kelso. As the receptionist answered, she seemed surprised to hear from Harv. He told her he needed to speak with Dr. Kelso right away. She told Harv that the Dr. was with a patient and would call right back. As Harv waited, he called his lawyer Steve Morris. He got through quickly because Steve was wondering what the heck had happened. He told Harv that he had received some of the notices stating that something was going on with Harv's assets because he was ill. That had been some time ago. Harvey briefly filled him in and asked for a late afternoon appointment, which was immediately granted. Harv told him he would tell the whole story once they were together at 4:30.

Once Harv closed the call, the phone rang. It was Dr. Kelso. Harvey quickly briefed him on what was going on and wanted a letter from his physician that he was capable of living independently and that his physical and mental health was good. He said, "Tom, I know you're busy, but I need this very quickly. You'll need it too because it is likely that either the authorities or the administration of Wildstone will ask you." Tom responded that he didn't have too many rounds to do at lunch, so if Harv could come by at 11:45, he would see him.

Next, he took a deep breath and used his phone to get the Illinois State Police, Division of Criminal Investigations (DCI) phone number. He made the call and asked for Special Agent Nolan Wilburn. The receptionist asked Harv his business. Harv briefed her and mentioned that he had met Special Agent Wilburn when his company was involved in designing and building the Springfield office. She told Harvey that SA Wilburn was the senior person in the office. She rang him through. Harv was pleased. The phone was answered after three rings, and Nolan answered, "Harvey, how are you. I remember we worked well together!" Harv responded that he recalled that also and congratulated Nolan on his promotion. "Just more paperwork," chuckled Nolan. "So why in the world are you reaching out to me?" Rather than go through the whole story on the phone, Harv briefed him on the main details and told him that The Team had more than ample evidence to prompt an investigation and would like to have Special Agent Wilburn and another agent or two come to his apartment the next afternoon to meet with them. "It sounds interesting. How about 3:00?" said Nolan. "Are you or the others in danger?" Harv said the chances were increasing as Anthony Culpepper and Charles Bilson were doing everything possible to save their skins. Nolan agreed and then said, "Stay safe and give us everything you've got when we get there. It'll be good to see you." "Roger that," said Harv as they hung up.

Harv had about 20 minutes left before he went to see the Dr., so he sat on the patio for a few minutes and gathered his thoughts. He also put his phone on the charger to make sure it was fully charged.

Harv walked into Dr. Kelso's office at 11:40 a.m. He sat down once he checked in at the desk. Within moments, he was called into one of Dr. Kelso's examining rooms by his nurse. Dr. Kelso came in. "Harvey, how the heck are you?" he asked. "It's been a little over a year. But I don't like what you told me. Please fill me in and remember it's all covered by confidentiality." Harvey replied, "Thanks for seeing me on such short notice, Tom." He then told Tom a brief version of the whole story about his illness, months in a coma, and then learning that his assets were gone once he became well enough to look into things. He also told Tom that he was ready to file charges. So, he needed to have credible evidence that he was fully mentally and physically capable of making his own decisions and living independently. He told Tom that it was likely that Culpepper would make it sound like Harv's life and health were at risk to find him and try to shut him up! Tom immediately got on board and gave Harv a full physical, including urine and blood work. Although the blood work results would not be available until late the following day, he found Harv to be amazingly healthy considering what he had been through. Dr. Kelso was also amazed that he had not been notified of his patient's Meningitis or hospitalization. He told Harv that he would renew his blood pressure medication and, once the labs were in, would write a statement of health and independence for Harvey and send it overnight mail to Harv and Attorney Steve Morris. Harv could also pick it up if he desired. He also promised Harv that all the information would be highly confidential. Feeling much better, Harv thanked him and promised to keep in touch both professionally and personally.

It was now 12:50 p.m., so Harv had time enough to head home. He made himself a sandwich for lunch and sat on his patio to eat.

Once he finished, he called Walt. He thought to ask Walt, "Are you being careful about what you say on the phone in case they're listening in?" Walt replied, "Almost always. I say almost because when you picked us up and called to tell me where you were, I didn't cover the intercom. I don't think that will make a difference." Harv told him he agreed. Then Harv brought Walt up to speed on what he had done and had planned with both his lawyer and the DCI. Walt told Harv to hold on a minute while he went to his patio outside. Walt said he would have the others at Harv's place at 11:00 a.m. tomorrow to gather all their information to turn over to Nolan Wilburn and to make sure they had time to run out and make copies if necessary. Harv agreed with the plan. He also told Walt that they needed to be incredibly careful. He recalled his call from Brenda and told Walt that they would never know who might be watching them for "Harvey's own good." Harv also said he would call Nolan to check if a welfare warrant of some kind had been placed with the Champaign PD. Harv did not want to be detained and turned in to Wildstone because they felt it was for his good. Harv felt if he were back at Wildstone, he would not likely survive. He also worried about Walt and Tory if somehow Culpepper found out that they were also involved! They both agreed that it would be better if Harv stayed away and let J.B. or Ted drive their rental car because nobody knew who it was. They said their goodbye's, and both were anxious and excited about finally bringing this forward to the authorities.

Harv had a couple of hours before heading to Steve Morris' office, so he took his dirty clothes to the complex's laundry facility. It was beautiful, and Harv was the only one there... at a little after 2:00 p.m. on a Monday, it was not surprising. He put his laundry in the washer, and while it was running, he called Nolan back. He didn't reach him this time but got his voicemail. He quickly said, "Nolan, it's Harv. I should have checked with you before, but I want to make sure that Wildstone has not placed any kind of look out for me, claiming that I am ill or need care. If they catch me, I'll be in trouble or dead! Please call me immediately when you know. Thanks, and I'll see you tomorrow." Once he made the call, Harv read a newspaper someone had left in the facility earlier that morning. After his clothes were dry, he headed back to his apartment.

He saw Marilyn along the way, and they exchanged greetings. Then she said something odd. "Harv, two men came in yesterday, and they were looking for you. They asked if Mr. England lived here. I told them that 'I would remember if he did,' and they took that as a no. Then they asked how much the apartments were, and I told them they started at $1,400 for one bedroom. They both laughed and said that England doesn't have any money anymore, nor do his friends. It was extraordinary, Harv. But I think I got rid of them." Harv asked her, "Did they show any credentials or badges?" Marilyn said that they produced nothing. Harv thanked her profusely and went back to the apartment. Once there, he folded his laundry, hung up his shirts and pants, and sprayed them with "Wrinkle Release," a trick he learned from Margaret. All the while, he was thinking who could be looking for him other than the authorities.

Soon, Harv's phone rang, and it was Nolan. "Harv, I'm glad you called me. I always want you to feel safe. I checked with Champaign PD, and there is not a BOLO for you for any reason." Harv thanked Nolan and told him that two men were at the complex yesterday asking the office if he was there. He recalled his conversation with Marilyn. Nolan said she did well. Together, Harv and Nolan figured that Culpepper had Wildstone Security trying to track Harv down, and they were probably visiting lots of apartment complexes. Harv took the opportunity to tell Nolan that he had gone to the doctor to get physically and mentally cleared and would have a letter soon if Culpepper tried to do a fast one. Nolan complimented Harv and told him he was doing everything right. "You're anticipating Culpepper's likely avenues to grab you and keep you from any type of testimony. We'll see you tomorrow. Be careful."

Harv headed for Steve Morris' office. Steve and Harv had been friends for years, and Steve had been involved with England Projects, LLC contracts, and dealings for a long time. He even represented Harv when the business was sold. He knew Harv and his style well. As Harv entered Mr. Morris' office, he noticed that it had been repainted and some new furnishings were on display. When Steve came out to the waiting area to meet Harv, they gave one another a man hug and proceeded to Steve's office. Harv, in fun, chided Steve for having fancy new furniture. Steve then ribbed Harv back by pointing out the pieces that Harv's business had bought for him. Then the conversation got right down to business. Harv outlined his "journey" from becoming ill to present. He showed copies of all the paperwork, including The Team's notes, document copies from Ted and J.B., even the photos from Charlene showing Harv's lamps and the image of Harv's mustang in Culpepper's garage. Steve called his assistant into the office. He asked her to please make copies of everything for him and even had Harv promise to share the tapes with him. Then Harv told Steve the reason for his visit and its urgency. Steve listened carefully and asked Harv why he wanted him to do it. Harv responded that he desired Steve's "agency" not to reveal his address and phone number to Wildstone. Steve agreed it was an excellent tact and proceeded to have Harvey sign a letter giving Steve his Power of Attorney only for these tasks. Steve said he would have a courier deliver Harv's message to Wildstone, end his care there, and have the courier certify delivery. He also promised to endorse the letter from Dr. Kelso to forward to Wildstone, and send the letters to Social Security and the Brown and Root pension office, having them now send Harv's checks to his new account. Harv told Steve that he and The Team would be meeting with the DCI tomorrow afternoon. Steve was so impressed with their actions he asked, "Are you and your friends, Private Investigators? You need to get your license and help others with such problems." Harv was flattered but said, "Let's get through this one first." After both agreeing and Harv getting his original paperwork back, he headed home.

Harv thought, "Tomorrow after Culpepper gets the letter from Steve, and then once we meet with the DCI, things will get very dicey quickly." It had started to rain, so even though he had a ball cap in the car. He stopped by Kohl's to pick up a rain jacket and an umbrella. He knew he'd discover other things he needed as time went by. Then he headed home.

This was to be a calm evening but with lots of anxiety. Harv made himself a chicken breast in the skillet, some mixed veggies, and a dinner salad with Ranch dressing and some cherry tomatoes. He ate quietly. After dinner, he rinsed the dishes, put them in the dishwasher, and put the food away. He thought he would wash dishes tomorrow when he had enough to be worthwhile. He watched TV for a while and then read from a Patterson novel. He went to bed, both tired and anxious, at about 10:30 p.m.

He woke up early and decided to get a workout in before he ate something. He headed over to the excellent fitness center and spent 45 minutes divided between the treadmill, stationary bike, and free weights. He then did his morning push-ups, sit-ups, and leg lifts. He felt tired when he got back to his apartment. He cleaned up and had some melon, a three-minute egg, and a piece of toast for breakfast. He found that it was just right.

He, knowing that The Team was coming at 11:00 a.m., headed out first to Walmart. In the electronics department, he was able to print the photo of his Mustang from his phone. He also made copies of the recordings, both from their interviews and even the recording Charlene had taken from Culpepper's office. On the way home, he went to Office Depot and made copies of the relevant documents. While at Office Depot, he received a call from Dr. Kelso's office, letting him know that his letter was ready. Harvey figured he could pick it up before going home, so he asked them to give him three copies. He picked up the documents, dropped one at Steve Morris's office, and headed to his apartment. Then something strange occurred. He was running a tad bit late, and he noticed that he was following his friends in J.B.'s rental car north on Prospect. But the car that was immediately between them was intentionally following J.B. Harv watched as J.B., not to be fooled, took an amazingly fast right turn from a left turn lane across traffic and sped into a neighborhood east of Prospect. The car following them was blocked by traffic in the right lane and could not follow. Harv watched and laughed as the driver and passenger threw a tantrum in the front seat. Harv took a picture with his cell phone camera. He then pulled into a Mobil station and called Walt. Walt answered, and Harv told him what he had observed. He suggested that they go north for a bit and then come south to his apartment. They agreed and ended up arriving nearly together. Once in the apartment, Harv texted the picture to Nolan and asked if it would be useful. He did not receive an immediate reply.

Harv put out some cold cuts, chips, and a dish with carrots, celery, and ranch dressing so they could "graze" as they reviewed and prepared. He then presented the picture of the car and men following J.B. and asked if either of them seemed familiar and received a negative answer. Walt suggested that if Nolan could identify the vehicle and people, it would be useful. Next, they discussed their approach to Nolan Wilburn.

First, Harv had gone to the "guest office" at the Baytowne complex and written synopsis of his "journey." The Team reviewed it and emphasized Harv's miraculous recovery that was utterly unexpected, and how Harv's first day awake included a visit from Anthony Culpepper. They also decided to emphasize that nobody expected him to live. Then they put a timeline together that included Harv beginning to exercise and use PT, how he developed a friendship with Brenda, and how he met Walt and Tory. They explained how he discovered that someone had taken all of his money and possessions and how Neil Goldman had found the original business sale account that with a substantial sum had not been stolen because it had not been found. They then were able to include Adam's assault with a syringe (which was later tested to contain Potassium Chloride), the dinner that had been laced with the same, how they interviewed people, and finally how Ted and J.B., both seasoned investigators, uncovered evidence of the forged Power of Attorney, bank documents and Harv's home sale. They then worked on estimating Harv's total economic loss, which was approximately over a million – seven hundred thousand dollars. That amount could be somewhat accurate because they had investigated the bank documents and those that supported Harv's house's sale to the Rochelle's.

The general furnishings of his home could only be estimated. All of this was not including the personal tragedy of the loss or the hardship, time, and effort that would be required to normalize Harv's life once the investigation has been satisfied. They also had the videos from the banks showing someone who looked like Bilson presenting the Power of Attorney to take possession of Harvey's money. Tory suggested that they ask Nolan to inform the Illinois Department of Public Health to have them work with them on an investigation of Wildstone. They agreed it was a good idea.

Then the conversation turned to safety. They had seen the men following J.B. and the others. They also knew that, by now, Culpepper would have received Harv's check out papers from his attorney and that Brown & Root, as well as Social Security, would redirect Harv's payments to his account instead of an account where Culpepper and Bilford could embezzle it. They decided to ask Nolan what he recommended.

They took a brief break from the conversation, knowing that Nolan Wilburn and another agent were likely to show up soon, and they had to make the most of their time together.

Harvey suggested to them his earlier thoughts of providing a safer environment for Walt, Tory, Ted, and J.B. He said that Tory could have the downstairs Murphy Bed and the private bathroom with a "roll in" shower and the things she needed. Tory was entirely independent if the facilities were appropriate. He and Walt could use the second story bedrooms and baths, and Harv would pay for motel rooms for Ted and J.B. They all could temporarily sign out from Wildstone because they were "going to visit relatives"; Tory to Ted's, her "nephew's" and Walt to J.B.'s. They needed to do so with no notice. They should pack first and load their things into J.B.'s and Ted's rentals and then simply drop their sign out notes at the office just before they left. This way, it was too short notice to have people following them. No decisions were made, but the idea was floated.

A little after 3:00 p.m., Special Agent Nolan Wilburn and Special Agent Scott ("Skitch" as he was called) Sullivan arrived. They knocked on the door to Harv's placed and he let them in. They were both casually dressed. After introductions, they went outside and sat on the covered patio. Harv first apologized for only having one copy of the information for Nolan. Of course, Nolan said he could produce more document copies quickly. While Nolan was enjoying seeing Harvey again, it was apparent that he did not suspect the significant web of deceit that had occurred. After listening to the story and seeing the evidence that had been discovered, both Nolan and Skitch wanted to listen to the recordings. While they were listening, Harv brought some soft drinks to the outside table. Everyone was dead quiet. Then Nolan spoke.

"This is a powerful story of several crimes against Harvey and maybe against others. You have brought us a complete case that we cannot ignore. Thank you. While some of the evidence you presented cannot be used in court because it would require a search warrant, the information contained can and will be used." "I agree," said Skitch. "I believe we need to understand what kind of trouble Culpepper and Bilford were in that predicated the crime against you, Harv. Motive matters to the courts. With that plus the recent crimes, you should be worried about your safety because these men may be willing to do anything to keep you all quiet."

Tory said, "Yes, you're right, Skitch, but we're not sure that they know about Walt's and my involvement; much less that both Ted and J.B. are investigative reporters."

Nolan responded to her directly. "Earlier today, just before I left my office to get here, Harv texted me the photograph of the two men in a car who were following you. I checked the license number and got a hit right away. The car is registered to Bilson's law firm. These men work for the law firm as investigators. We must assume that they knew who they were following and why. Also, being investigators, they may carry badges and guns, so people are likely to respond to them as authority figures. You must stay safe."

Harv told him of his idea to move them in with him. Nolan thought it was a good idea. He then asked if Harv still had his carry permit. Harv replied that he did, but his weapons were all gone with his home. Nolan sent Skitch to the car to retrieve a pistol. He then advised Harv to speak with Marilyn and get her to assure her silence about his whereabouts.

Skitch returned with an older but very nice Smith & Wesson .38 special revolver in a holster with some additional ammo. Nolan slid it over to Harv and said, "This is my personal weapon. It's no good unless it's loaded and with you!" Harv nodded.

Walt then asked, "So gentlemen, how long do you think this will take to have them arrested and make us safe? Much less, get Harv's stuff back?" Special Agent Wilburn replied, "I have no idea, but your information will make the process much faster than normal. Before we take any action, we will have to subpoena the financial records for Wildstone here in Champaign, and then our forensic accountants will have to identify the malfeasance and crime. We need that to prove the motive for the crime. We will then involve the Illinois Department of Public Health to identify any other wrongdoing by Culpepper and Bilson. The bank videos showing Bilson presenting the forged Powers of Attorney along with the statements of the bank managers will be important. In my opinion, we must keep this so quiet until we can get a search warrant for both Culpepper's and Bilson's properties and bank records to see what we can find... possessions, the Mustang, artwork and any paper trail that helps us. We'll also gain access to both of their accounts. I'd say a month or longer. And then once charges are brought, it'll take a while to go to court. We want confessions from both of them so the process will be faster and easier. However, remember that both Culpepper and Bilson have worked for Wildstone for years and have many contacts who might whisper in their ears about an investigation going on. It's hard to keep things quiet. And, because of the crimes, they may take desperate actions to try to save themselves."

Skitch added, "Once charges are brought, it's likely that Wildstone will terminate both of them to avoid an even larger scandal. It's also likely that with what they did, they will be arraigned quickly. We will ask to have them monitored if they are released on bail. I think you'll be safe within a couple of weeks, but we will keep in regular touch."

"We may want to 'quietly' let Wildstone corporate know that both Culpepper and Bilson are under investigation and that no harassment of any resident will be tolerated ...and that we'll be watching. But not before getting search warrants for their personal properties. Otherwise, the likelihood of us recovering your lamps, artwork or Mustang goes way down because they will likely hide them."

Harv told everyone that this was a productive meeting, and all agreed. Nolan suggested that they would be welcome at any time to help them. As they left for their office, Nolan reminded Harv and all of them to be careful. He also told them that The Team's job was done. Now the DCI was stepping in!

They all sat back with a big sigh. The game was on! Harv suggested that everyone should go with J.B. back to Wildstone and pack their clothes, meds, books, and other necessities, and write notes signing out of Wildstone for family visits, Tory's to Connecticut, Walt's to visit friends. Harv also recommended that they take their computers and give their apartments the "once-over" because it might be that Culpepper's goons would go in to look for anything they might want. Then they could return to Harv's after 8:30 when it was dusk, and they were less likely to be seen. They decided to bring some takeout dinner with them so they could all eat when they arrived. While they agreed to the arrangements, Walt called Marilyn in the Baytowne offices.

When she answered, she told Harv he just caught her leaving for the day. Harv asked, "This may be a bit unusual, but do you have a two-bedroom that you would rent me for my friends to stay maybe up to a couple of weeks?" Marilyn surprised him by saying, "Yes, we do. When people are shopping for places to live, especially in more upscale housing like ours, they often want to try it for a bit before they commit. It's unusual to have them stay for a couple of weeks, but I can arrange it. I have an apartment for them; it's not nearly as nice as yours, but it'll be good. It's just upstairs near yours. Can they climb stairs?" Harv answered in the affirmative and rented it on the spot. She said she would bring two keys by on her way home. That was easy!

Harv turned to the others and told them what he had done. They were all pleased. They would be all together, and it would be cheaper than a decent hotel. Besides, they had the fitness center, a pool, Harv's covered patio and the other amenities. Everyone was pleased.

J.B., Ted, Walt, and Tory left to gather their belongings. Harv made sure that the rooms were ready, and bathrooms stocked with towels, washcloths, and paper goods. He checked to make sure the Murphy Bed was made, had blankets and that everything was ready for both Walt and Tory. He wanted her to be incredibly comfortable. Then he went to the dining room, checked out the revolver, which was much like his own Colt Trooper .357, made sure it was loaded and placed it in the drawer in the front entryway just below the security monitor. He heard a soft chime from the front door camera and noticed Marilyn approaching. He was there as soon as she rang the bell. She handed him the keys to the apartment upstairs for Ted and J.B. while he thanked her profusely. He poured a glass of red wine for himself and went out on his patio to relax and think about things.

Game On!

The Team was back at Harvey's around 8:45 p.m. and Walt and Tory put away their things in their rooms. As they did that, he handed Ted and J.B. each a key for their apartment upstairs. They ran upstairs just long enough to drop their bags and return. Both commented on how nice it was.

They then went out on the patio to eat Mexican takeout that they had brought. Harv served wine and beer and turned on soft lights so they could see to eat yet enjoy the pond lights and fountain.

After dinner, everyone refilled their beverages and sat back to have a relaxed conversation. Ted suggested that it was good to have a real investigation starting with agents who were not only good at their jobs but also now friends. As they agreed, Tory stated that they still needed to stay low and be careful. Harv responded that while that was true, he would check with Brenda and Charlene in the morning to see if anything was up. Tory volunteered to call Charlene while Harv called Brenda. As they were talking, Harv received a call from Marilyn. "Hi, Marilyn," Harv said. "Is everything OK?"

Marilyn replied, "So far it's fine, but after I left you, I noticed two men checking out your car and writing down the license number. There are several lockable garages on the other side of the building you may have seen." Harv acknowledged that he had. Marilyn went on, "Garage number 4 is open. Please get your car in there and lock it. The electronic keypad number is 0225 then 'enter'. To close, it's the same. I'll give it to you for free because you're renting two apartments. I'm worried about you. I will not reveal that you're here and I'll tell the other employees to keep their mouths shut too."

Harv thanked her and hung up. As he related the call to the others, J.B. said, "I'm the one they wouldn't recognize. I'll put your car in the garage. While I'm out there, I'll check around for them." As he took Harv's keys and proceeded to put the car in the garage, the others were concerned. "If these are Bilson's guys they are trained investigators and will be able to track the license number to you, Harv," Walt said. "Marilyn did the right thing to offer you the garage."

When that was said, they all discussed the possibility that Culpepper had received Harvey's "sign out letter" from Steve Morris, was suspicious and felt the loss of control. It was logical that it might have caused Culpepper to call Bilford and get his investigators involved. What worried them was if not to harm or threaten Harv or any of them, why would they be looking for them? At that time, Harv reminded all of them of the security cameras that worked with both the front door and the patio door. Ted said, "If someone knocks on the door and you can't see them on the camera, do not answer. It simply means that the person has disabled the camera for nefarious reasons." Harv agreed and showed everyone where the pistol was kept.

By now, J.B had returned. Harv suggested that both J.B. and Ted should park their rental cars at different buildings away from Harv's apartment. They agreed and left to re-park their cars.

They joked that they had become very suspicious people while they finished their drinks. Then J.B. and Ted went upstairs to their apartment while Tory, Walt and Harv readied themselves for bed.

In the morning, Harv dressed in his workout gear and awakened Walt. Walt whined about waking up early to work out before breakfast and Harv teased him until he got out of bed and got ready. They headed out to the facility health club. They worked out for about 45 minutes then Harv set out for a mile run this day. Walt joined him but was not happy about it. It was a little after 8:00 a.m. when they got home. Tory was up but was still in her robe. She greeted them with an admonishment to let her know when they left and when to expect them back. They agreed as they said, "Yes, mother!" Harv cut up the rest of the melon and made some English Muffins and scrambled eggs. They ate their breakfast and passed around sections of the News Gazette they had picked up at the health club. There wasn't much conversation, but they knew there would be plenty to talk about later. Harv went to clean up for the day while Walt washed the dishes and Tory headed back to the bathroom.

At about 9:20, Harv and Walt were cleaned up and dressed and had another cup of coffee while they sat on the patio. Harv had not been so inclined before, but they decided that whenever they left the apartment, they should use the unique locking bar on the sliding glass doors and close the draperies.

As they were finishing up their coffee, the doorbell rang. The security camera showed Ted and J.B. waiting at the door. Walt let them in. J.B. said, "You got any coffee here? How about some breakfast?" Harv laughed, and Tory, now at the table said, "Just like boys!" Harvey put on another pot of coffee, and Walt started some scrambled eggs and English Muffins. Everything was done in a few minutes, and Ted and J.B. were very thankful. "You guys will have to do the dishes," Walt said. Both Ted and J.B. nodded while they ate. As that was going on, Harvey went onto the patio to call Brenda. Tory went into the small office nook to call Charlene. Both took notebooks.

Brenda was so pleased to hear from Harv. She told him to hold on while she got to a private place. Once there, she greeted him excitedly. She told Harv that she received a note, as did the Duty Nurse Glenda, that Harvey England had checked out of Wildstone and would not be returning. The note came from Anthony Culpepper's office, and he stated that he would be checking to see if any of Mr. England's belongings were still in his old room. Brenda also told Harv that she had picked up his clothes and personal items from his room and could meet him somewhere to return them. They agreed to meet at Veterans' Bank right after her shift at 4:30 p.m. Harv told her that if she thought she was followed, not to go. Brenda then told Harv that she heard that Culpepper was behaving very differently; he had yelled at people, he told people not to ask him anything and was even edgy and nervous instead of his usual "in charge" persona. She made sure to say that she had not witnessed it but had heard it around the facility. Harv asked her if she felt threatened or unsafe. Brenda told him she didn't feel unsafe in any way. Harv said that this was one of the reasons he did not tell her where he was. He did ask Brenda to be very aware of who might be following her or listening to her conversations. She assured him she would be careful. They both thanked each other and confirmed their 4:30 meeting at the bank.

Harv came back into the apartment. Shortly after, Tory emerged from the office nook. Both related their news to the rest and Walt took notes. As Harv described his conversation with Brenda, their most significant concern was that she would be followed by one of Culpepper's or Belford's "goons". They agreed that one of them would go with Harv to meet Brenda. Then it was Tory's turn.

Tory told about a remarkably interesting conversation with Charlene. When she first called, Charlene said that she would call Tory back and hung up. A few minutes later, Charlene called Tory back. She was whispering and said she had gone to the bathroom and had checked the stalls to make sure nobody else was there. She told Tory that Mr. Culpepper was infuriated when he received Harvey's official notice from the attorney that he was checking out of Wildstone. Also, then he received a registered letter from Dr. Kelso, showing that both in-depth physical and psychological examinations proved Harvey fit to live independently. Culpepper called both the attorney's and Dr.'s offices to find out where Harvey was living, but they would not tell him. Charlene said that he had then called Bilford who had come over right away. She said she listened to a little of the conversation until Culpepper shut down his intercom. Bilford told Culpepper that for Harv to have gone to his attorney and Dr. he must have suspected that they might try to bring him back under the guise of Harv's inabilities to live independently, so they could no longer use that as a reason. He also may have told them about his money and house being gone. The solution was that an "accident" had to happen! Charlene was so worried that something terrible was going to happen. Both Culpepper and Bilford had left together right after their conversation muttering about who they needed to call. Charlene cut off the call because she had to get back to her desk to avoid suspicion.

They sat down and talked about it, recognizing that the two culprits were going to be acting quickly to avoid investigation and capture. Little did they know that it was already underway!

Midst of the Storm

At 4:15, J.B. driving his rental with Harvey headed for the bank. They were there before Brenda and watched her pull in. As she got out of the car, two men approached her. Harv was pretty sure they were the two he had seen following J.B.'s car before. They pulled badges and began to ask her questions. Rather than revealing themselves, Harv immediately called Brenda's cell phone, and she surprisingly answered. Harv told her quietly that the two men were private investigators employed by Bilson and they could not require her to tell them or show them anything! She thanked Harv gratefully without identifying him and hung up. Then J.B. and Harv watched her step back, point her finger and yell at them. She screamed at them to leave immediately and punched 911 into her phone while they were watching. They shook their heads, and Harv and J.B. watched them drive off. Harv called Brenda and recommended that she go into the bank and wait for him. She did so. Harv put a hat on, pulled it low on his face and slowly moseyed into the bank. He took the grocery bag with his things from Brenda and, after agreeing to talk later, he went back to the car. He had also advised Brenda to do a couple of other "errands" while she was out. Brenda headed for the grocery store while J.B. and Harv followed her at a significant distance. Yep, after about a half a mile, the car that Harv had seen following J.B. pulled out after Brenda. They all followed Brenda to the grocery store and watched while she walked to the pharmacy at the end of the plaza. Then she headed home with purchases in tow. They watched the investigators leave the plaza before they headed back to the apartment. They both felt that Brenda's strength in the situation kept her from submitting to an unlawful search, a search of her cell phone, an interrogation, or another such outcome. Both Harv and J.B. wondered what they wanted; they agreed probably Harvey's location was their goal.

As they arrived at Baytowne and searched out a parking place for J.B.'s rental, they immediately knew where Bilford's goons had gone. They recognized the car outside of the offices. Harv immediately called Marilyn, who answered. He asked her if they were there, and she replied, "Why yes, Mr. Smith." Harv then told her that they were indeed not police and she had no obligation to comply. He asked her if they had threatened her, and she replied, "Yes to that also." Harv said that J.B. and he would remain hidden outside and call if she needed help. They said goodbye and Harv and J.B. remained in his car. The two men came out of the office and looked angry. They listened, and one of them said, "Who is training them? Can't be those old people!" But, rather than leave, they walked down around Harvey's building. J.B. immediately called the apartment and told them to get inside and close the door and blinds. Then as Harv and J.B. watched, the two men wandered around and looked at all the license plates, taking photos of some of them. Then they walked around the patios by the pond. Those who were outside waved nicely to them and they waved back. Not finding what they wanted, they left. Harv and J.B. went home. The others asked what had happened, and J.B. recalled the story to them while Harv took his belongings and put them away. As Harv came back into the living room, he made the mood less favorable. He said, "I realized that I used this address on my new car registration. Even though my old address is on my driver's license, when I bought the new car, I used this one. If they're smart, they will soon have my address." "Can they get it?" asked Walt. Ted replied, "Absolutely, yes. They even sell them to marketers for all the junk mailings. Also, if they know one police officer, they can get it soon. We hope that because Harvey's purchase isn't long ago, the records haven't been updated yet. They can take months to update."

Tory looked thoughtful and asked, "With the investigation under way, what do they want with you? What could they do?" Ted answered saying, "Several things. They may not know yet that there is an investigation. They want to know what we know, who we've told, what evidence we have and who we've given it to. Once they know that, Bilford and Culpepper can threaten or hurt us to keep us from testifying, they could pay us to call off the dogs or, if they believe they'll get caught they can destroy evidence and even go on the lamb." "So", Tory said, "They won't stop trying as long as Culpepper and Bilford think they can help themselves." They all agreed to that. They also agreed to let everyone know if they were going anywhere, to always have their phones with them and to keep doors locked. Going in at least pairs would also be advisable.

Harv called Nolan Wilburn. He answered and told Harv he was just going to call him. Nolan said the DCI agents were working fast. They already had warrants for Culpepper's and Bilford's personal bank accounts and investments, and for Wildstone Champaign's business financial records. His forensic accountants were going through the personal records as they spoke. Tomorrow they would start on Wildstone's. Harv related what had happened with Bilford's investigators. Nolan told Harvey it would get more dangerous because likely tomorrow they would advise Wildstone of the investigation and tell them to release the records per the warrant. "Once that happens," Nolan said, "the worry will really show." He told them to be incredibly careful.

Harv related what he had just been told to the others. He recommended that this was probably the last evening they should spend on the patio. Blinds closed and patio doors locked after this for a while! Walt suggested that, rather than cook their own food, they save it and have Chinese food delivered to them and eat at a leisurely pace on the patio for the last time for a while. They thought it sounded good so put in an order. As they waited for it to be delivered, both Ted and J.B. went upstairs to their place to check in with their clients and the Globe.

About 30 minutes later the bell rang. Thinking that it was Ted and J.B., Tory was ready to open the door. Walt grabbed her and put his finger over his lips and motioned to the Video screen. Two men, unknown to them, were standing in front of the door. Walt motioned to Harv to come over to see if they were the same two who had been following them. Harv nodded. At the same time, Ted and J.B. came down the hallway and kept going as though normal. The phone rang a moment later and it was Ted. He warned Tory who answered the phone not to open the door. She whispered that they already knew. Harv slipped the .38 from the drawer. They waited. The doorbell again rang, and Walt started the recorder. Harv asked, "Who's there?" The answer was "Federal Agents, open your door." Harv demanded that they put their badges and creds up to the peephole. One of them quickly flashed his badge but not long enough for Harv or the others to see it. He said, "Slower and longer please." One of the men said, "I told you who we are, so let us in." Harv refused. The man was more than irritated as he said, "You'll be sorry!" Harv told the others to stand back. He opened the door and faced them as he drew the .38 from his waistband and cocked it. The two looked at him and the quiet one said, "We'll get you old man!" Harv innocently asked, "For what? Tell me one illegal act me or my friends have done?" They both smirked and threatened him again. Harv began to slowly bring up the weapon and the men left quickly. Harv then carefully dropped the hammer of the revolver.

Ted and J.B. rounded the hallway. They had been waiting in secret in case their help was needed. Once they knew Harv had taken care of things, they stayed hidden to protect their identities. As they came in the door, the food was delivered. Ted said, "You've just dealt with enough. I'll pay for it."

"Thanks," said the others. Once they were on the patio, Harv still with the .38 in his waistband, Tory asked him, "Would you really have used it?" Harv looked at Walt who replied, "Without question, he would have if they had either drawn a weapon or tried to force their way inside." Both Harv and Walt chuckled. Walt then drew from his right front pocket a small Ruger .380 LCP that he carried. Tory said, "Isn't that against the rules at Wildstone?" Walt nodded and smiled. "I have a permit to carry and we aren't at Wildstone!" They then began to eat. J.B. went inside and brought out a nice, chilled bottle of Riesling and a Cabernet for Harv and Ted. After a half hour or so they were relaxed. Tory stated that she felt that the investigators may try to harass them, but neither was anxious to lose his license for Bilford or Culpepper so it was a low likelihood that they would try force to get to The Team. They agreed but would be careful.

Without anything being said they were all wondering about tomorrow. Would Culpepper's and/or Bilford's bank accounts show suspicious activity? Would they be able to find problems with the Champaign Wildstone records? Would they find significant deposits they could link to Harv's assets? Tory had an idea that she felt she should run by the others. She asked, "If Culpepper or Bilson get wind of the audits on them and Wildstone, might that cause either of them who have any of Harv's property like the photos that Charlene took, to hide it to avoid being caught?" "Good comment, Tory," Harv said and then stated, "I'll call Nolan first thing in the morning so he can get a head start."

J.B. and Ted both said that by tomorrow a.m. if not before, Culpepper and Bilford would know of the investigation and that they were being watched. If they were likely to make mistakes that would work against them, this would be the time due to panic or fear. Then both of them admitted what everyone knew. "Once this is over and the resolution has been made, Ted and I will be writing a series of stories on this situation for The Globe," said J.B. "That's our payment and it's what we do. We will protect the names as we must, but this story will grab the hearts and minds of millions. It makes us wonder just how many such situations either smaller or larger with which seniors have had to deal. And how many have not found any resolution."

"Take Walt, for instance," said Tory as she gestured toward Walt. "I've known him for years. He didn't have lots of cash, so he turned in everything he owned to Wildstone for the apartment for himself and Debbie; and now has not enough left that would enable him to move out. I wonder just how much of the money they got for his assets actually were required for his apartment."

"That's worth looking into," said Harv. They all nodded and agreed. Harv continued, "While what happened to me is really bad, I'll bet it's not the first time. There may be a number of people who, due to their lack of cognitive senses or due to a lack of family or both, have been deceived and robbed by Culpepper and Bilford or those like them." Tory went on, "You're probably right. I'm not blaming Wildstone, but both Culpepper and Bilford work for Wildstone so Wildstone would be responsible." Nodding heads prevailed. "That's a next step to investigate," said Walt. "Not just for Wildstone, but for all of our seniors who are living in senior communities at all levels of care."

Answers are Forthcoming

The next morning, they went about their tasks as normal. Harv was up early and chastised Walt until they both took off for the fitness center. Walt had his .380 with him. They went through a workout routine and headed back to the apartment. The two "investigators" approached them, blocked the sidewalk and one said, "Tell us what you know and who you've told! Now!" Walt put his hand in his pocket but hesitated. Harv stood eye to eye with the one who was obviously the leader and said, "Show me your Federal credentials." The man hesitated, and then pulled out his private investigator's license along with the Bilford law firm's I.D. "I thought so," said Harv. "You'll get nothing from me!" The other man grabbed Harv's shoulder to restrain him and Harv let go with a roundhouse to the left side of the man's face. The investigator went down hard. As the other man stepped forward, Walt pulled the pistol from his pocket and advised him to stop. The one then helped the other up and they stood in front of Harv who said, "You think you can take my home, my money and my belongings and then tell me not to do anything? You are idiots! We're capable and will not be intimidated!" Then Walt and Harv walked off.

When they got back to the apartment, they got a cup of coffee and Harv called Nolan. He was not available, so Harv left a message. He drank his coffee and went to clean up. He came out of the bathroom feeling like a new man. He was mentally and emotionally passed the skirmish of the morning. He was just telling Tory, while Walt was in the shower that he was almost ready to call Bilford and tell him to call off his dogs, but that he would ask Nolan first. As he was finishing his statement to Tory, the phone rang. It was Nolan.

"Harv I need to make this clear in a hurry. We found almost $400,000.00 missing from Wildstone Champaign's coffers in February with no explanation. It was replaced in April with again no explanation. We know it was your money. We also found that both Culpepper's and Bilford's personal saving's accounts had deposits of just over $300,000.00 each which we suspect was also your money. We're working on Wildstone's books, but we've got a search warrant for both Culpepper's and Bilford's homes to check for your belongings before they get wind and try to hide or sell some of your stuff.

Please start by meeting us at Culpepper's place in one hour. Do you know where he lives?" "I do," Said Harv. "Good. If you do not see my car, do not make yourself known. Make sure my team is in the house first. Understand?" "Absolutely, Nolan. I'll see you there."

As the two disconnected and as Walt emerged, Harvey told them what had just transpired. They were all anxious and excited as they waited the 40 minutes before they would leave. Tory called Ted and told him to get J.B. and meet them at Harv's. They were there promptly and were informed of the call. They decided that only Harv and Walt would go into the house. After all, Harv was the only one who knew his own belongings and many of those were marked with Margaret's initials. The others would go in a separate car to wait and observe. Harv parked his car almost a block distant from Culpepper's house because he saw no sign of Special Agent Wilburn's vehicle or others. Walt looked at his watch and then at Harvey as he said, "We're almost 20 minutes early." Harv replied that he was just anxious to get there. They waited impatiently while the minutes went buy. Exactly on time they saw Nolan's interceptor version of a gray Ford Edge roll up to the door.

Four other unmarked official vehicles rolled up behind him. Nolan pulled into the driveway, blocking it off. The others blocked the end of the drive and parked along the curb. Nolan, along with two others approached the door. Harv and Walt rolled down their windows to listen. They could see more than hear the loud knocks on the door. When they heard Nolan announce, "DCI Agents. Open the door!" two other agents trotted around the back of the house to insure nobody decided to leave by the back door. In a moment Culpepper answered the door and was handcuffed and taken into custody. As he was being led to one of the cars and put into the back seat, Harv received a call from Nolan. He said, "Harv we're all clear. Come meet me at the front door." Harv asked if he could bring Walt and was told not at the present. Walt waited patiently in the car while Harv went to the door. "Harv", said Nolan, "you have only one task and that is to identify any belongings that are yours. If you see something, you may not touch it but point it out to me. We will record it on camera and then you will tell us how you know it is yours. Got it?" Harv simply nodded and said, "Yes, I understand." Then Nolan handed Mrs. Culpepper, who was terribly disturbed and crying, a copy of the search warrant. He turned to her and said, "I know this is an awful surprise for you. I suspect that you did not know what Charles was doing, but we'll save that discussion for later. You may watch us, but you may not, in any way, interfere. Do you understand?" She gave him a nod. He then said to his two other agents and camera person, "Let's do it."

Harv was both excited and sad to find that some of Margaret's and his belongings were here in this house. Nolan stated, "Harv, we will look at areas of the house in an organized fashion. If you see something that is yours in that area only, tell me, we will take movies and then I will pick it up and you will then confirm that it's yours. I will then put a small piece of marker tape on it and it will then be handled by our forensic people. You will receive it from us once it is verified and logged; could take a week or a month. The 'chain of custody' has to be perfect." Harv nodded.

They began their organized and slow walk-through. Mrs. Culpepper dabbed tears and sniffled throughout the search. On the first hallway table, Harv pointed to a medium-sized, hand-painted porcelain vase. He told Nolan, "Margaret bought it in Italy." The vase was documented on camera while Nolan picked it up. "Look underneath, Nolan," said Harv. Nolan turned it over and underneath the base they saw very small initials "ME" for Margaret England. It was tagged and they moved on. Harvey explained that Margaret had always chuckled that her initials spelled "ME" so she marked all of her valuable items with the initials either on the item itself or on a small label affixed to the item as to not lesson the value. Nolan chuckled and remarked that he wished everyone were so organized.

As they worked slowly through the house Harv found many articles of art and all three of the original Tiffany lamps, a Tiffany desk light and desk set that all belonged to Margaret and him. In Culpepper's study they found a model of his mustang, a couple of M.C. Escher's smaller artworks and a small but fine pen collection that were Harvey's. They even found a couple of cookbooks in the kitchen that were signed by Margaret. Finally, they made it to the garage and there was Harvey's 1965 red Mustang convertible. Several tools and even repair manuals for the mustang were recovered. It was a good day. Nolan turned around to Harv and said, "Even without over a million dollars of theft of your money and home, what we've found here will put him in prison for 30 plus years. How much are the Tiffanies worth?" Harv replied, "I haven't researched them lately but at least $30K each." Nolan nodded, then went on. "One of the reasons we took Culpepper to the car was that we did not want him to warn Bilford that he's next. Can you follow us over to his place?" Harv said, "Can't wait, Nolan." Nolan told him that it will be the same procedure and not to come until he gets the call. Harv agreed.

Harv got into his car with Walt and waited for Nolan and his group to leave for Bilford's place. They noticed that Culpepper was being charged and taken into custody. The car with him inside drove away. Harv recounted the story of the search of Culpepper's house and what they found initially. Walt said, "You know, Harv, if it weren't for Culpepper's greed and his desire for your things, he would have avoided this part. I'm sure glad they found the Mustang." Harv agreed and told him what Nolan said about the theft of the items alone. As Nolan left with his team, Harv and Walt followed.

Bilford lived out of town a bit toward Mahomet on a nice several-acre piece of land. The DCI agents and uniformed state troopers followed the same procedure. The major difference was then Bilford, being a lawyer, became irate and asked to read the search warrant before allowing them to proceed. Nolan gave him the papers and then handcuffed him and took him to one of the cars. Bilford's wife was not home so the agents began their search. Harv got the call and went to the front door. As he passed by the car with Bilford, he could hear Bilford screaming and cursing at him. As he looked at Nolan, he held up his index finger as to say, "Just a moment." He then turned to Bilford, smiled broadly, and did a little shuffle before turning and meeting Nolan at the front door. Nolan was laughing as were his agents.

They again went through a painstaking search of his house. It was a little larger than Culpepper's and more traditional with a few more antiques. In the Parlor, they found an old candle table that was Margaret's, an original Stickley rocking chair, an antique Persian rug and, in the bedroom, an ornate, large oriental style jewelry box with most of Margaret's fine jewelry including pieces from Tiffany, Cartier, a Rolex watch her father had given her and many more valuable and beautiful pieces. It would be later revealed that Bilford told his wife he had gone to an antique auction where he had purchased them. In the basement workshop they found a few of Harvey's tools. When they were done, Harv admitted to Nolan that some things like dishes, doilies and the like would be hard for him to identify. Nolan understood and said that they would also go through absolutely everything for Margaret's "ME" labels. Nolan released him and told him to take Walt and go home and he would call as soon as he could.

Nolan winked at Harv and said, "With your help and that of Walt, Tory, Ted and J.B. we've got this! I'd hire you if I could. Thanks. By the way, you'll have no more problems with Bilford's investigators. The firm will be either sold off or closed by the end of next week."

Harv went to his car and told Walt about what had happened. They drove home stopping by Steak n Shake on the way. They were hungry. Of course, they got enough for everybody and headed home.

Tory, Ted, and J.B. were anxiously awaiting as Harv and Walt arrived. They immediately went to the table as Harv and Walt pulled dishes out for them to use for their food. Harv brought out both a chilled Chardonnay and Merlot while Walt got glasses. They all joked about eating like at the Ritz but quickly settled into their meal. Tory asked, "So tell us what happened. We're all curious. Was it a good day for you and us?" Harv, who was munching away on a double steak burger and fries asked them to wait until he was done eating, then he and Walt could talk all about it. When all of them had overeaten, they sat back, refilled their glasses and J.B. poked at Harvey saying, "It's time big fella ...tell us the scoop." And Harv did just that.

He told them he felt much better about things. First, he gave them examples of his property they had readily identified because of Margaret's labeling obsession. He then told them what Nolan had said about the stolen property alone, landing them in prison for a long time, much less the huge sums of money Culpepper and Bilford had stolen. When asked if Culpepper and Bilford reacted the same, Harv told them of the differences. Walt just had to tell them about Harv's taunt of Bilford that had Nolan and the agents laughing. Walt also mentioned that they would have no more problems with the investigators. It was all summed up by Harv saying that Nolan said he would call soon. They were all anxious for that call.

Tory asked Harv, "Seriously, Harv, none of us have actually asked this, but how are you feeling now?" Immediately, Harv's reactions were hard to read. Then his eyes became a little teary. As he spoke, his voice for the first time since they had met him was a bit shaky. He said, "Since Margaret died, I have never felt deep friendships. Then when I first awoke from the coma and learned everything was gone, I felt so very lost and wronged. But then I began to heal and met Walt who reminded me of caring and humor and friendship. He also taught me that I was tough enough to move forward. Then you, Tory. You are among the most brilliant of people I have ever met, and you accepted me. Then Ted and J.B., meeting you through Tory has meant so much. And then for you all to take on this investigation with me made me feel alive. Now that we are approaching the conclusion, I don't want it to end. I believe The Team has a place for doing good work! Thank you all." In a rare moment of openness and clarity, they all felt the same way. It was close to a group hug ...then Ted raised his glass and said, "To the Team!" They all echoed, "To the Team!"

Then they moved to the living room and Tory, being the analytical mind, asked about what they had really done and the skills they developed and used. They talked it through and determined that they had worked together without dissent and listened well. They doggedly tracked down all the information available to them and used the skills of both Ted and J.B. whose investigative reporting skills and talents abounded. They even made it through the attempts at intimidation and even danger. They avoided being viewed as a threat to Culpepper and Bilford by identifying the listening potential through the intercoms. They also stood up to significant intimidation. They were proud of themselves.

They all went to bed pleased with the day.

The Outcomes are Clear

Four days later, after an unhurried workout and a run around Baytowne with Walt taking up the rear as they got home, Harv and Walt hit the showers and cleaned up. Tory was already up and had baked some homemade biscuits. As Harv came into the kitchen, he told Tory to call Ted and ask them to come down. He put 10 sausage patties on the griddle to cook. Then he cracked 10 eggs, added some milk and whisked them all together. He waited until the sausage was almost done before pouring the eggs into the skillet to cook. He took the cheddar cheese from the fridge and now was all prepared to have sausage, egg and cheese biscuits for breakfast. As Walt set the table, they were all ready. Harv's phone rang.

It was Nolan. He asked if he could come by in a half hour. Harv said sure if he was in town. Nolan laughed and said he'd been in town most days until this case was solved. He also said that because he worked in Zone 5 for the DCI, he was always close. They agreed on a half-hour. The Team enjoyed their breakfast and coffee and wondered what Nolan had to tell them. J.B. brought up the fact that he and Ted would be focused on writing the series of articles on the investigation so the Globe would get the "scoop" on any other newsgroups. They would have to leave soon and head back to Boston. They felt this would be a big story. With "the graying of America," the numbers of older Americans were growing at historic rates. In fact, J.B. said, the July 2020 U.S. Census reported that the 65 years old plus category had grown more than 34% over the last decade. No other age group grew at this rate. And they were likely living longer due to attitudes toward health and new discoveries and treatments. They felt their article would certainly increase the need for transparency from senior living communities, nursing homes and various care options even including limited home care solutions. Harv piped in by saying, "I'll bet the whole senior care industry will be wetting their pants once the national media gets ahold of your story!" They all chuckled until Walt said, "I don't mean to burst anyone's bubble, but this is serious stuff. Just think, if Harv had died like was forecast, an over a million-dollar theft would probably have happened; and what about so many who do not have a group like us to help them? I am just so pleased we came together on this. How many families and individuals are told when their relative passes that all of their assets were used for their care when it's really not true?" They all nodded. Tory was just ready to start more discussion when the doorbell rang. Harv noticed it was Nolan and readily opened the door.

They exchanged positive greetings, and Nolan seemed upbeat. He came right in, sat down at the table on a chair from the patio and then asked Harv if he was going to offer him some coffee. Harv asked, "Can I offer you a cup of coffee?" They all chuckled, as Nolan said, "Sure. Thanks. Just a little cream please."

As Harvey delivered it, Nolan began to speak. "I'm filling you in on all that I know so far. You cannot repeat it to anyone," he said while staring directly at J.B. and Ted, "until the information is ready to be made public. J.B., Ted, I have reported to my superiors that you guys get an exclusive for two weeks to give you a chance to decide how you'll handle this and write your articles. You may even want to write a book." Both Ted and J.B. smiled as did Tory. Nolan went on. "First of all, Harv, we have recovered only a few pieces of furniture as you know but were able to identify some additional items that had the famous, 'ME' labels on them. We must hold them until the case is fully adjudicated, then you'll receive them back. Because of its size and unquestioning ownership, we will deliver the mustang to you sometime in the next few weeks with a corrected title. It will come on a flatbed, and you will receive a call telling you when to expect it." Harv smiled very broadly and rubbed his hands together. "Thanks, Nolan," he said. Then Tory asked, "Can you tell us about the rest of the case?"

Nolan took a drink of his coffee and smiled. "This is a lot of information, so Ted, J.B., if you want to take notes, please do so. You already know much of it. I will get you the full report once we're ready to release the story. Let's see, where I begin. OK, first, our audit of Wildstone Champaign's books revealed no wrongdoing. They showed that the shortfall we told you about came from withdrawals signed off by Culpepper. When confronted, both he and Bilford confessed. We were able to coerce them by saying that if they confessed to the original crimes, all white-collar, we would not prosecute them for the attempted murder of you, Harv and maybe you too Walt, or for the break-ins, or for the intrusions of their listening devices through the intercoms, etc. Both broke down and told us that they had invested heavily in a new pharma company that was supposed to do record business. That is until COVID hit. They lost the money and needed to pay it back before Wildstone discovered it. Harvey was the perfect fall guy. He was supposed to die, had no family but had lots of money in his house, décor, and investments. By Bilford forging the Power of Attorney documents, which by-the-way he admitted after seeing the bank videos, they were able to take possession of and liquidate your property, Harv. Once they sold the house, they donated most of the furniture to a not-for-profit agency, making themselves look so generous! But they needed a little more, so they divested of your investments, checking and savings accounts. Because there was more than was needed to give back to Wildstone, they just kept the rest for themselves. Both have been fired from Wildstone, both have been arraigned in court and will plead guilty to avoid the public embarrassment of a trial."

The Team really got quiet for a moment. They took sips of their coffee and thanked Nolan profusely. Tory told him that without the good relationship they shared, they could not have worked with law enforcement to a common goal. Nolan nodded. Harv, Walt, Ted and J.B. all echoed the appreciation and gratitude. Then Walt said, "Nolan we thank you. But this all started with us trying to help Harv get his life, home, belongings, and money back. How can we do that?" Nolan smiled and continued. "Skitch and I sat with senior representatives of Wildstone who flew in here for private conversations once Culpepper's and Bilford's wrongdoings were revealed to them. After discussions directly with them, they have agreed that the negative publicity that would be caused by you suing Culpepper, Bilford and Wildstone to try to regain your assets would cause them great long-term harm to their finances and reputation. Plus, Culpepper's and Bilford's lawyers would take most of the money. Wildstone has agreed that if you will accurately and honestly tell them what you have lost, that they will pay you a full settlement, reimburse the costs paid for months of care plus a significant additional amount to cover all of the suffering and months of your investigation to bring us to this conclusion. They also said they would cover the lease on the apartment until you find a suitable home and for the automobile, you had to buy because of the loss of your truck, which by-the-way, nobody can seem to find."

"That sounds more than fair," said Harv. "How long before I'll get the settlement." Nolan said, "I really don't know, but they said it would be within 30 days of your submission. Your list should be comprehensive because you won't get a second chance." "I can do that," Harv stated. "Harv, when you estimate your investigative time, don't forget to include 'payment' for Walt, Tory, Ted and J.B. Also, remember that your 'pain and suffering' should be substantial. Most people wouldn't get into this kind of mess for millions of dollars." Harv agreed and asked, "When should I have my list ready, and who should I give it to?" Nolan answered, "Present it to me because we will have to record it as a compensatory settlement. The amount will be kept confidential so none of your friends, acquaintances or people in the community will know anything but that a settlement was reached. If asked, you can simply say that you lost everything and Wildstone did their best to help you. I must say that they are more than fair. We don't need everybody knowing your private finances and business."

"So how will Wildstone get its money back?" Asked Tory. Nolan went on to tell them that not only does Wildstone have significant insurance, but that they would, once the settlement was reached, sue both Culpepper and Bilford. The courts would ultimately rule in Wildstone's favor so they would recover something, but it could take years in the court system. Ted said, "Wildstone is being very fair, but to be honest, it serves them well. It protects their reputation rather than fighting it and ultimately losing millions upon millions of dollars in the long run." J.B. said, "Amen!"

Nolan ended his discussion with, "I'm so glad you folks were here to help. In fact, as I've told my colleagues, the case was complete when you called me. You had the crime, the perpetrators, and the evidence ready to go. We would love it if all the P.I.'s and consultants we dealt with were so efficient, didn't care about receiving credit, and worked cases that mattered. Just contact me when you're ready to submit your settlement. Please don't wait too long. You know where to reach me. We will be in touch. I really need to get going now." Everyone thanked him and shook his hand in spite of the COVID. As Nolan was ready to walk out the door, Harv said, "Hold on a moment." He reached into the drawer below the security monitor and pulled out the .38 special revolver. "I believe this is yours," Harv said and handed it to Nolan. Nolan smiled and said, "Thanks. I've missed it. Glad you didn't need it!"

The Settlement

The next week was very anticlimactic, and in some ways even boring. On Tuesday, everyone helped Tory move back into her apartment where she could have her own place, wash her clothes, have her things around her and have her services delivered by Wildstone. The people there, especially the employees, treated her like royalty because The Team's outcomes solved so many management problems at this location of Wildstone. She knew that she, Harv and Walt would be in regular touch, but she missed them and their closeness during the storm of the investigation.

Wednesday, both J.B. and Ted returned to Boston. They were extremely excited to write and publish their "scoop" and knew, without a doubt that it would be of national interest. The Editor was also excited about it. The hardest thing would be keeping it under wraps until it was released. They had promised to let Nolan see it before its release just to ensure the correct and accurate information would be presented.

Now it was just Harv and Walt. They were both great company for each other. Walt wasn't that keen on moving back to his apartment, but it was, after all, next door to Tory. Harv asked him to stay on until he had compiled his submission for compensation, and Walt readily agreed.

Over the next few days, Harv, with Walt's help, listed everything they could think of while being fair. The settlement for Harv's property, cash and investments were $1.6MM; then came care at Wildstone of $75K, Harv's apartment lease for a year, $22K and investigative costs of $20 K per each of the five on The Team. Harv added pain and suffering of $250K. In addition, Harv tried to estimate the amount of his pension and social security that had been taken. He felt bad about the amount because he would have been pleased just to get his money and the cost of his home back. He called Nolan, who stopped by and took a look at his submission for reimbursement. He pocketed the paperwork and said he let Harvey know soon.

The next day Nolan called as Harv and Walt had a quiet breakfast. In fact, they were both commenting on just how much too quiet it was. "Good news, Harv," said Nolan. "I faxed your submission to Wildstone, and we discussed it this morning. Your list was for a bit more than $2.1 mil. You were out over a million and a half so none of us was pleased with how little you'd receive for everything you've gone through. Knowing that you'll likely share this with the others, even though you are the one who was wronged, Wildstone will write you a check for an even $3.5 million dollars by next week. I hope that this helps in a small way to compensate for your trouble, aggravation, investigation and the loss of so much." Harvey was again gob smacked. "I don't know how to thank you, Nolan. Walt and I were actually just discussing how quiet our lives are right now. After the last couple of months, it is too quiet. I think we'll go over to Tory's and discuss when Walt will move home."

Nolan asked, "Will you call me when you're there, please?" Harv didn't ask him why but said, "Sure. I'll do it." Nolan told Harv that was good and that he'd look forward to it, said till then and hung up.

Harv wondered to himself what he would do with the money and if he should even tell Walt, Tory, or the others how much he would get. Nolan was right; Harv was the one who was wronged. But without these special people, the outcome would have been very different. Walt broke in, "Earth to Harv, earth to Harv; come in Harv." Harvey laughed and then told Walt about the conversation in general. Harv and Walt were both pleased by the outcomes, even though Harv did not share the total amount with him. Harvey kept thinking to himself, "How is Walt better off now? Or Tory? What should I do?" Those thoughts weighed heavily on his mind.

Harvey and Walt had another cup of coffee for a late a.m. pick-me-up. While Walt looked through a Motor Trend magazine, Harv plunged deep into thought while scribbling on a pad at the kitchen table. He felt much better after his thought time. He noticed what Walt was reading and asked, "Is your driver's license up to date?" Walt said, "I really don't know; let me look." He looked in his wallet and said, "It expires in two months." Harv then asked, "So what kind of cars do you like?" Walt answered, "I really prefer mid-size trucks like the Toyota Tacoma's. You like 'em?" Harv answered in the affirmative. He said, "I've always preferred trucks, but for hauling friends like Tory and you, the Edge was better." Walt then said, "Wish I could afford one. Then I could come and go as I pleased." Harv's mind was then made up!

At around 2:00 on that Thursday, they headed over to Tory's place. Even though it had only been a few days, they had missed one another. They hugged and said hello and then went onto the patio. It was there that Harv broke the news to them. He told them that each of them would get $150,000.00 for the investigative work to bring down Culpepper and Bilford once he received the settlement check. Both Walt and Tory were aghast at the amount! Harv insisted that it was only fair because he couldn't have been able to proceed without them. He also said he would send a check in the same amounts to Ted and J.B. Tory warned him not to do so. While they were of great help and consequence, they were formally working for the Boston Globe and being paid well for their time so they could not accept any other payment due to conflict of interest. Harv understood. They enjoyed time rehashing some of their interesting encounters over the last couple of months and then Harv remembered he needed to call Nolan. He made the call, and Nolan answered, he asked Harv to put him on the speaker. Harv did so, and Nolan said, "Congratulations to all of you and thanks. The good news is that none of this happened because of Wildstone, and they are working hard to make up for it including a generous settlement for Harvey." They all agreed verbally. Nolan went on; "I just wanted you to know that if you're bored and want something worthwhile to do, I can help you to get Private Investigators' Licenses and, believe me, we have some good cases we could use your help with solving. Just think of how many situations like Harv's that happen every year? Let alone, every month? Think about it, will you?" The Team smiled at each other and collectively said, "We'll call you back very soon!" Nolan left the call and they were almost laughing. "I'm in," said Harv. "Me too!" announced Walt. "Who's going to take care of you if I'm not there?" "Count me in," exclaimed Tory. They all decided The Team would continue to make a positive difference!

Over the weekend, Walt packed up his clothes, and he and Harv prepared to move him back to his apartment on Monday. Harv was off in his own little world and making phone calls. Walt wondered what was going on. Over the weekend, masks on their faces, they went shopping for food and picked up some wine; oh yes, they needed wine. They enjoyed a movie on TV and had a few glasses of wine, finishing on the patio looking onto the pond. "Gonna miss this view and space around us," said Walt. Harv replied, "It sure will be different without you around." They headed off to bed and slept well.

Monday morning came, and Walt made omelets, one of his specialties that Harv had not yet tasted. Onions, bacon, green peppers, sharp cheddar cheese and some sausage, made these special. He served them with English Muffins, and Harv was hugely impressed. They both ate too much and settled back with a cup of coffee. Walt said, "I've gotta tell ya, Harv, that I'm not looking forward to being alone at Wildstone. We have had too much fun and adventure for that. Not to get too sappy, but having a friend is so good." Harv jumped on that comment and said, "Me too. I like to be bored sometimes, but without somebody to eat with, travel with and all the other things, it would get very lonely. Although you certainly can't replace Margaret, it's been good to have you here, buddy! And you make great omelets!" Little did Walt know what was to come. Walt threw his suitcase into Harv's Edge, and they headed to Walt's place. As they arrived at Wildstone, Walt started to retrieve his suitcase. Harv said sharply, "Leave it. We'll get it in a minute." Because of his stern tone of voice, Walt complied without argument. A couple of parking spots to the right of where Harv parked was a dark gray Toyota Tacoma Quad Cab Limited with chrome mirrors, wheels and running boards. Harv walked over to it, and Walt followed. "Real pretty truck, huh," Walt said. Harv reached into his pockets, retrieved the keys, and unlocked the truck. "It's got leather, JBL stereo and GPS too. It's even got the 4-wheel drive." Harv said. Walt looked confused. Harv turned and handed the keys to Walt. "It's yours, Walt." Walt, in shock, actually cried. The tears dripped from his eyes as he hugged Harv. He had not felt as much emotion since he became a widower. "I can't accept this from you. It's too much," he said. Harv smiled and said, "It's not enough. Now let's go into your apartment, get the rest of your stuff, load it into your truck and get back home to Baytowne."

Walt was beside himself. As they went through Walt's little apartment at Wildstone gathering and inventorying his belongings, Harv told Walt, "If you think you can handle it, I'd like you to move into the guest bed and bath in my apartment. Over the next couple of months, I'll be looking for a house to buy and it will have plenty of room for us. We're smart enough to give each other space when we need it, but if we're working on a case in the future, it'll be good to be close. Plus, there's plenty of room for Tory to come over. Once you are out of here, you'll get your pension, your social security and with your share of the case proceeds, you'll be able to actually live life rather than pay for your Wildstone expenses. I think it will be good for both of us. What do you think?"

Walt could only smile, nod, and swallow hard!

Acknowledgements (SO MANY)

With immense love, appreciation, and admiration for my dear wife of 52 years, Becky, who has supported me throughout the process (and, in fact, helped with the characters)!

To my children Todd and Sara who are wonderful encouragers!

Thanks to Mr. Clay Culpepper, Esq upon whose advice I leaned!

For the Cover: Mr. Wendell Amos representing Harvey England.

Mr. Walt King representing Walt Schell

The Reverend Janice Keebler, Ret., representing Tory Randall

And, to the wonderful Photographer, Kathy Smith of Townsend, TN!

Thanks to so many friends who came to mind as I wrote this book. I have used some part of their names (but not the whole) because they are and have been important in my life. Please keep in mind they are all wonderful even if their name represents a villain! All these people have been very important to me as have been many others whose names partial or complete I have not yet used (yet)!

I decided not to list them because it may violate their privacy, or I might forget to mention a special someone.

To God Be the Glory!

About the Author

Carl Goodman was born in Urbana, IL. After a couple of years in college he was drafted and became part of the U.S. Air Force. He is a proud veteran Staff Sergeant with two Air Force Commendation Medals, a Presidential Unit Citation, the Republic of Vietnam Campaign Medal, and the Vietnam Service Medal among other decorations.

Upon his return from Southeast Asia to the U.S. and discharge from the service, his family moved to Indianapolis where they lived for 8 years. Carl sold pharmaceuticals and medical supplies for 2 ½ years while the family saved money so he could return to college. He graduated from Eastern Illinois University with a concentration in Labor Relations and an excellent academic record. Carl speaks reasonable German and Thai and is very interested in languages. Post-graduation, they remained in Indianapolis until they moved from there to the Rochester, NY area in 1981. After 26 years in New York State, Carl and his wife, Becky, moved to Tennessee in 2007.

Since his college graduation, Carl has been a Human Resources professional with a focus on the issues that surround employment, staffing and lawful practices. After working for one of the finest, high-profile companies in the world for fourteen plus years, he founded his consulting firm, The ISAAC Network, LLC in 1994 and is still working in his field (as well as fulfilling the writing "bug").

Carl has been married for 52+ years to Becky and they have two "wonderful, terrific, successful and loving (other positive adjectives may apply)" children, Todd, and Sara. Carl and Becky live in the Smoky Mountains of Tennessee in a small and peaceful community.

Made in the USA
Monee, IL
30 May 2021